THE 13TH FLOOR

FLOOR

A Ghost Story

YEARLING BOOKS are designed especially to entertain and enlighten young people. Patricia Reilly Giff, consultant to this series, received her bachelor's degree from Marymount College and a master's degree in history from St. John's University. She holds a Professional Diploma in Reading and a Doctorate of Humane Letters from Hofstra University. She was a teacher and reading consultant for many years, and is the author of numerous books for young readers.

For a complete listing of all Yearling titles, write to
Dell Readers Service
P.O. Box 1045
South Holland, IL 60473

Sid Fleischman

THE 13TH FLOOR

A Ghost Story

Illustrations by Peter Sís

A Yearling Book

Published by
Bantam Doubleday Dell Books for Young Readers
a division of
Bantam Doubleday Dell Publishing Group, Inc.
1540 Broadway
New York, New York 10036

ISBN: 0-440-41243-9

Reprinted by arrangement with Greenwillow Books, a division of William Morrow & Company, Inc.

Printed in the United States of America

May 1997

10 9 8 7 6 5 4 3 2 1

CWO

For Betty,
with happy memories

Contents

CHAPTER 1

Voices

The phone lit up and began to warble. I was watching an old Tarzan movie on TV, studying for a test in Spanish, and baby-sitting the kid next door. I could also chew gum at the same time, except that I didn't have money for trifles.

"The phone's ringing, Buddy," said Hayley, who was sitting on the stairs and drawing pictures of horses with long yellow manes. She was the kid next door, with long yellow hair.

Sometimes I answered the phone, and sometimes I let the answering machine get it. Lately a girl from school, a girl everyone called Garbo, was stalking me. Could that be her now? I liked her a lot, but she was into weight lifting. I wasn't crazy about having a girlfriend who had larger biceps and deltoids than I did.

The phone rang again just as the Lord of the Apes began to bellow out his jungle yell. I grabbed the phone to shut it up.

"*¿Hola?*" I said, trying out my Spanish.

"Buddy, don't you ever answer the phone?" It was my grown-up sister, Liz. "I knew you were home."

"I thought it might be the stalker calling me."

"That cute girl with the sunglasses in your theater group?"

"And my Spanish class. She has me surrounded."

Liz was about a thousand years older than me. She was twenty-three and just out of law school. She wanted to specialize in legal aid for poor people, and her first case had made her kind of famous. A neighbor had charged a harmless old man in Chula Vista with having the "evil eye" and causing flowers to wilt every time he looked at her garden. Liz came up with the curveball defense that it was *not against the law* to wilt flowers by looking at them. She won the case and made the evening news all over the country.

The trouble with being a hotshot in legal aid is that Liz hardly earned parking meter money. Now that we were orphans, we needed some big bucks. It wasn't that we were broke. It was worse than that. We owed a gasping ton of money.

Liz was saying, "Maybe you're not answering the phone in case it's someone calling about buying the house."

"Maybe," I muttered.

"Buddy, you know we need to raise money. We've got to sell the house."

"But we grew up here. My room is *my* room. This is *home*."

"I'm sorry, Buddy," she answered. She must be hurting as much as I was, I thought. She just wouldn't show it.

The big old stucco house had been in the Stebbins family since way back in the Dark Ages. It must have been around 1910 that my great-grandfather had come out from Massachusetts and opened his law office on India Street. Then he'd built this house on a hill above Old Town. I guess he'd liked the airy view of the ships going and coming in San Diego Bay, and so did I.

He also liked to hold spirit meetings in the garden at night among the orange blossoms and pepper trees. Liz told me they were called séances. He'd lift a ship's old copper speaking trumpet to his lips and command the dead to talk. He claimed that sometimes they answered back—once through the spout of a brass teakettle in the kitchen.

"But the Stebbins house is haunted," I said. "No one's going to want a home with ghosts in white sheets running around and voices whistling out of teakettles and chains rattling."

"The house is *not* haunted," Liz snapped back. "There are no ghosts, and when have you ever heard chains rattling? Don't start any crazy rumors, Bud."

"Do you think our great-grandfather was a nutcake?"

"Nutcake is neither a medical nor a legal definition," she said.

"Liz, we're not in court. Do you think he was balmy?"

"I think it just amused him to believe he could talk to ghosts. You remember how much fun it was to believe in the Easter Bunny and the Tooth Fairy."

"But I was only four or five."

"Perfectly sane people can be slightly mad," she conceded, laughing.

"I wonder why anyone would want to rap with the dead. It would give me the cold chills."

"You mean to say you don't know?"

"Know what?"

"He was trying to contact an ancestor from way, way back. The ghost of a sea captain." She paused and then snapped her fingers. "Crackstone—that was his name. Yes, Captain Crackstone."

"Who was he?"

"A dashing pirate."

My eyes must have popped. A pirate hanging from our family tree? A genuine, bloodthirsty buccaneer? I was thrilled. "Why didn't anyone tell me?"

Liz seemed surprised that this family lore had slipped past me. "Captain Crackstone was hardly table conversation anymore, Buddy. He lived almost three hundred years ago."

"Did he have men walk the plank and bury treasure and things like that?"

"I don't know about walking the plank," she replied. "But he'd buried a treasure somewhere. Crackstone was the name he used only when he was flying the skull and crossbones. His real name was Stebbins. As a direct descendant our great-grandfather hoped to coax the captain into revealing where he'd buried the loot. After all, the riches would be useless to a ghost."

"Did Captain Crackstone ever turn up in the garden?" I asked.

"Not so much as a foggy wisp. The only thing of his that has come down through the generations is that battered ship's trumpet."

"Maybe I'll give it a try," I said.

Liz broke into a small laugh. "Tell the captain that if he buried some treasure, we need the money." Then she said, "I know it's my turn to make dinner tonight, but would you mind fixing your own? I've got to balance my checkbook."

"That could take you all week," I said. Liz was smart, but not with numbers.

"G'bye, Buddy dear."

Hayley had been so quiet on the stairs, drawing wild palominos, that I had forgotten she was there.

"Are you moving, Buddy?" she asked, looking up.

"What gives you that idea?"

"The For Sale sign out front. I can read, Buddy."

I nodded.

"Where will you live?" she murmured.

"We're thinking about the jungle. We could live up in a tree and swing on vines."

"Like that dumb movie? How come Tarzan never washes his hands before he eats? He never even brushes his teeth."

"Here comes your mother."

Hayley was so easy to baby-sit that I didn't like to accept pay for it. But the way furniture and stuff was disappearing from the house, I knew that Liz must be getting panicky about money. She didn't think I was old enough to be responsible for anything but keeping my room clean. Baby-sitting made me feel that I was helping to pay my own way a little. Tomorrow I had a lawn to cut down the street.

At the door Hayley gave me a shy look and said, "I don't want you to move away, Buddy."

"I'll come back and see you all the time," I said.

I'd lost interest in the Lord of the Apes. I hurried upstairs and found the ship's trumpet in my father's study. The copper was still bright, but it had more dents in it than the fender of a used car.

I couldn't help giving it a shake, as if to empty it of any old leftover voices.

I took a breath and held it to my lips.

"Captain Crackstone! Ahoy! This is me, Buddy Stebbins! I guess I'm a descendant of yours! Can you hear me! Liz sold the teakettle, so don't try talking through it. Now what about that treasure? Where'd you bury it, sir?"

CHAPTER 2

A Message from Abigail

I walked through the house, calling out to the pirate ghost, until I caught sight of myself in the downstairs hall mirror.

"Buddy!" I shouted through the trumpet. "Stebbins, you look like a nitwit! You're balmy! You're a nutcake! Your porch light has gone dim. Do you really expect some three-hundred-year-old ghost to hear you?"

I returned the trumpet to my dad's cabinet. If it were possible to talk to the dead, I ought to have called out to my mom and dad.

They had been killed in a small plane crash across the border in Mexico. It was months before Liz broke the news to me that our father, a private dealer in early Mexican art, had left a lot of debts.

"We'll have to pay the money back," Liz had said.

"Sure." I'd agreed. "Of course. Positively. How much?"

"Big bucks."

"How big?"

"Not to worry, Buddy."

"I want to worry, Liz."

"The money we get for the house will square everything."

"Can't we just keep selling stuff?" I asked.

"But we're running out of family heirlooms." She gave a little laugh. "We may have to sell off your model airplanes next."

I hardly missed the old china dishes and silver serving pieces that we never used anyway. But of course, I'd noticed when the dining room table and chairs vanished. I was kind of sorry now that Liz had managed to sell the heavy brass teakettle, in case—just in case—some spirit tried to talk out of the spout again. Again? Aw, it probably never happened in the first place, I reminded myself.

The phone rang again, and I thought it must be Liz calling back to remind me to turn on the lawn sprinklers. It was May and hot winds were blowing in off the desert and everything was turning dry as sandpaper. I turned down the sound on Tarzan and said, "Me, Buddy."

It was a girl's voice. A new girl in the drama club at school.

"How dare you tell everyone I'm stalking you!"

I swallowed hard. So much for my nutty fantasy. "Hello, Garbo," I said. I imagined her flaming hair shooting straight out like something in *The Bride of Frankenstein*, which I'd seen last week.

"I didn't tell everyone," I protested.

"And I don't keep calling you up! This is the *first* time I've ever called you."

"Would you like to rehearse our parts for the play?" I asked boldly. I could understand the drama club's letting her in, but I think the only reason I got past the door was that the school needed someone to play Ichabod Crane in *The Headless Horseman*. I was tall and gangly enough.

"Or we could study together for the test in Spanish," I added. "It's better to have someone to study with. Especially for a test."

"And I hardly lift weights *at all!*" Garbo said, and slammed down her phone.

I felt myself blush. I'd never had anyone hang up on me before. It was embarrassing. But she'd become personally aware of me at last. Never before had she taken any more notice than absolutely necessary.

I turned on the lawn sprinklers before I forgot. Then I went around back to water my mother's roses. I checked the bay, to see if there was anything out there. I counted three submarines gathered like suckling pigs up against a gray navy supply ship. But the big stuff—the aircraft carriers and cruisers—was out to sea.

I could hardly believe it when Garbo called back. At almost thirteen years of age, I guessed I was not old enough to understand women. In a voice so sweet it must have given her cavities, she asked if I understood how to translate the paragraph on page 162 in our Spanish book. So I changed into my new tennis shoes with their green glow-in-the-dark laces and got my bike out of the garage. I hurried through the lawn sprinklers and raced over to her house. We studied together for the test, but her mind seemed to be a million miles away. Light-years away, in fact.

"What's your sign?" she asked.

"I don't know. Saturn, I think."

"Saturn is not an astrological sign."

She figured out that I was a Pisces, which didn't seem to please her a great deal. Then she got the newspaper and consulted the astrology column. It said that Pisces should beware of birds that flock together.

"What do you suppose that means?" she asked, biting a fingernail.

"Maybe it means to run for cover when seagulls fly over," I said.

"That's not funny."

"I wasn't trying to be funny," I muttered, sounding a lot like Liz. "I was only trying to be mildly amusing."

She wasn't mildly amused, either. It was clear that she took astrology as seriously as appendicitis and that I'd better change the subject. In addition to the zodiac, she was heavily into cosmetics. It didn't leave us much to talk about. I found myself sneaking a glance at my digital wristwatch.

"Do you always wear sunglasses at night?" I asked.

"Of course," she said. "I'm studying to be a movie star."

By time I got home, my crush on Garbo was history. There in the entry stood Liz, soaking wet. In long green pants she looked like a frog ready to leap. At me.

"Did it rain?" I asked, baffled.

"Yes, two months ago," Liz answered. "You merely forgot to turn off the sprinklers. I merely had to beat my way through a rain forest to reach the front door. I may merely murder you."

"Gasp!" I said. "I'm sorry, Liz."

She broke into a smile. "Actually, Bud, it's the first time all day I've felt cool."

She slipped off her shoes and got a bath towel to dry

off her hair. At first neither of us noticed that the red light was flashing on the answering machine. When it caught her eye, she crossed over to the table and pressed the playback button.

"Hark!" a girl cried out, in an accent straight from England. "Is it you, Mistress Stebbins? Is it you who knows the law from here to there and slam to pieces? Hark! Hark! A great calamity is befalling me. Help me! Make haste, mistress, to India Street! The Zachary Building. To the thirteenth floor! I'm Abigail Parsons, aye, your own relative herself! You'll know me by my best Turkey shawl and my starched white bonnet. Don't fail me!"

"The Zachary Building," I muttered. "That's where our great-grandfather had his law office."

"A clever touch," Liz said, cocking a skeptical look at the answering machine. She suspected fraud and shot me her best lawyer's cold-eyed, cross-examining gaze.

"Confess, Buddy. Starched white bonnet! Is this your idea of a practical joke? Who—whom—did you get to do the English voice? One of your friends at school? Garbo?"

I threw one hand in the air as if I were taking an oath. "I confess, Liz! I confess I didn't have anything to do with this. I don't even know what a Turkey shawl is. Furthermore, Garbo doesn't do accents. She does eyelashes."

"In that case—"

"Yeah, in that case, Liz, it sounds like some relative wants to hire you. Abigail something or other. I didn't know we had any relatives still alive."

"We don't," Liz answered. "And she's not. This is a

put-on, Buddy. Who's trying to put us on, and why? Therein lies the mystery."

Therein? She'd only begun using words like that since law school.

"How do you know it's a put-on?"

Liz brushed aside the question as if it were a mere piece of lint.

"Someone is setting up a simpleminded practical joke. It'll spring the moment I turn up at the Zachary Building."

"What joke?"

"The girl said she'd be waiting on the thirteenth floor, didn't she?"

"Yup."

"Buddy, office buildings don't *have* thirteenth floors. A lot of people are too superstitious to rent space on a floor with a bad-luck number like that."

I took a breath and nodded and smiled. "Yeah. There's a word for it."

"Triskaidekaphobia," Liz said as if it were a word she used every twenty minutes. "It means fear of the number thirteen. A lot of cities skip it when they number the streets, and they name the offending road something else. See? Superstition is ever alive and well, Buddy. I'm positive the elevator in the Zachary Building jumps from the twelfth to the fourteen floor."

"So if you turn up looking for Abigail, the laugh is on you."

"As laughs go, I'd rate it slightly below a snicker," Liz replied.

"Maybe it was one of your crackpot boyfriends."

"I don't have any crackpot boyfriends."

"How about the one who claimed to have been kidnapped by a flying saucer for six hours and eighteen minutes? Harvey."

"Ex-boyfriend," Liz said. "Don't remind me." Then she dismissed the telephone message with a wave of her hand. "And let's forget Abigail."

CHAPTER 3

The 13th Floor

Liz left in the morning for her office and didn't come back.

After school I cut the lawn down the street, tossed a few basketballs, and started my homework. It was not unusual for Liz to be late for dinner, but she always gave me a call.

I was having a little trouble concentrating on my Spanish, with the final coming up tomorrow. I hadn't done so hot on the last test and needed to make up for it.

Finally I turned on the radio and thawed a container of spaghetti sauce my mother had frozen almost a year ago. I heard on the news there was a monster traffic jam along the waterfront. Some truck driver claimed he saw real wet tears dripping from the left eye of a huge movie billboard of Elvis Presley. People were flocking from all over the county to witness the miracle or whatever it was. I wondered if Liz had somehow got trapped in all the fuss. I boiled up some pasta and ate alone.

When Liz didn't turn up by ten-thirty in the evening, I called the hospitals. Good news! They'd never heard of her. But where was she? Should I call the police? Missing persons?

I waited another half hour and called the police.

"What was she wearing?" asked the policewoman.

"I don't know. I was at school when she left."

"How tall is she?"

I didn't know exactly. "Kind of tall for a girl," I said.

"Weight."

"About average, I guess."

It embarrassed me that I couldn't give a better description of my own sister. Even though I saw Liz every day, I realized now how little I really looked at her. After all, she was only my sister. *Only?* She was the only person left alive who really knew I was alive.

The officer told me that Liz would probably walk in the door at any moment. "It's natural to worry, sonny, but don't let your imagination run away with you. Is there someone to take care of you?"

My mind raced ahead to awful possibilities, and I heard myself shade the truth. "Heaps of relatives, ma'am. Don't worry about me."

"Fine. Check with us tomorrow, sonny."

All our relatives had been put to rest in an old family record book upstairs in the glass-doored bookcase. There was no one left but the two of us. I missed not having cousins to run to, or aunts and uncles. We were alone, Liz and me. Just us. And what if I should lose her? For the first time I grasped the hazard I had run in calling the police.

I might be able to take care of myself, but to the police I was "sonny" and not quite thirteen years old. Without Liz I'd be thrown into an orphanage or something. Without her I was sunk. She was my lifeline.

In a sudden panic I dialed the police again to say that Liz had turned up and thanks a lot. But I hung up before the call went through. Dimwit. It's a great time to worry about yourself. Liz could be in major trouble and might really need the police.

It must have been about an hour before daybreak when I jumped out of bed. Could Liz have gone to meet that weird lady with the English voice? Abigail?

I ran across the hall to Liz's room. When I heard no sounds of breathing, I snapped on the light. The bed hadn't been touched. Liz was still missing.

The only thing out of place was a large book open on her desk. It looked as if she'd been browsing through the family births and deaths going back practically to Adam and Eve. My mom had always called it the Stebbins death book. Now, in Liz's own bold handwriting, she and my dad were the latest entries.

But Liz hadn't been looking at the last page. She had had the book open practically at the beginning where the old ink had turned as pale as tea stains.

A name in the middle of the page jumped out at me:

Abigail Parsons

Born, Northampton, Mass., 1682, seventh child of Mary Bliss and John Parsons. At age ten, tried as a witch in Boston, 1692–

I didn't have to read any further. I was dead certain that Liz had run down to the Zachary Building to check out the voice on the answering machine. Unless someone had stolen a look at the family death book, how could anyone have known we had an ancestor named Abigail?

I spotted my tennis shoes glowing in my closet and

pulled them on. I threw my Spanish book and some other school stuff into my backpack and jumped on my bike.

By the time I reached India Street, dawn was up and the big old windows of the Zachary Building were flashing a bonfire red. I was wearing my Walkman radio so I could tune in to the all-news station. I wanted to stay in touch with the world, just in case a body had been discovered somewhere.

The doors were still locked for the night, so I waited around for someone with keys to show up. I guess the building once had been the grandest in town when my great-grandfather had kept his office there. Now it was partly boarded up and looked broken down and tuckered out. If it had been a horse, I believe someone would have shot it.

To pass the time, I listened to some music on the Walkman and read the lettering on the windows. There was a bail bondsman, a chiropractor for dogs and cats, and an outfit that bought gold teeth. One of the corner bay windows had a flashing purple neon sign that said MADAME ZORITA, PALMS READ & FORTUNES TOLD. KNOWS ALL.

Knows all?

If she'd been in, I'd have been tempted to ask her what had happened to Liz. To save the money, I looked at my own palm. After a moment's close study, I came to the startling conclusion there was no way the creases in my hand could have jumped around overnight to clue me in to Liz's disappearance.

Wasn't anyone ever going to show up around here? I dug through my stuff. I'd forgotten I had a pencil flashlight in my backpack. I shook it, and it still worked. I fished out my pocket-size tape recorder and listened to myself practicing Spanish pronunciations. *"¡Es excelente! ¡Es estupendo! ¡Es magnífico!"*

Finally a lanky man wearing a leather bow tie turned up with a jangling ring of brass keys. He opened the doors, and I followed him in. After making a quick check of the directory on the wall, I called to him.

"Don't you have a thirteenth floor, sir?" I asked.

He turned with a curious look. For a moment I thought he might never before have been addressed as "sir" and didn't know how to deal with it.

"Kid," he said in a friendly drawl, "I declare if you ain't the second person who asked about that. Do we have a thirteenth floor? Can pigs fly? Someone's playing a joke on you."

My heart took a leap. "Was the other person a girl—I mean, a young woman? With large glasses? Yesterday afternoon!"

"That's her."

"What happened then, sir? Did she turn around and leave?"

"She turned around and stepped into the elevator. That's the last I seen of her, kid, going up. Now, I got things to do."

He vanished through a door, and I stepped into the elevator. The inside was a kind of reddish mahogany that must have once been kept varnished and polished. Now the panels were trashed, with names and pierced hearts and initials carved across the wood.

There were no buttons to push, but it was self-service. There was a framed sign telling you to push the hand lever in the direction of the arrows, forward or back, to the floor you viewed through a small window.

I shut the elevator door and pulled the handle back. Sure enough, the elevator began a slow creak upward. I pulled the handle back a bit more, and the elevator rose a little faster.

Through the window, hardly as large as a picture frame, I could see the passing numbers of the floors clearly painted in white on the wall of the shaft. When I reached the twelfth floor, I slowed the elevator to a crawl. I continued upward, inch by inch, not sure what to look for. But before long I saw the number 14 appear in the peep window. The thirteenth floor wasn't there.

I shoved open the door and stepped out to look around. The door closed itself behind me.

"Liz?"

There wasn't a soul on the floor. To judge by posters still clinging to the walls, there must have been an overall factory up here.

Before I could get back inside the elevator, it went clattering back down. The guy with the bow tie must have needed it. I waited a few moments and then rang to bring the elevator back up.

I got tired of waiting and decided to try the stairs. If somehow Liz had found a way onto the thirteenth floor, so would I.

I gazed about me carefully, step by step, feeling the walls with my hands. I hoped at any moment to trip a secret spot that would open a secret door. Something. Anything.

But nothing. When I came out on the landing, I found myself on the twelfth floor.

I rang for the elevator again. It seemed a month before it finally rumbled back to me. Once more I put my eye to the peep window to watch, inch by inch, for any change as we crept upward.

I saw something.

I stopped the elevator and peered hard. Had Liz seen it, too, that thin streak of yellow, like light escaping under a door? Was that it?

I jumped to the elevator door and pulled it open. There, staring back at me, was the solid, solid wall of the shaft.

I returned to the peep window. The light had slipped into view at the very bottom—and there it was again! My heart was thundering now, practically drowning out the music in my ears.

I tapped the elevator lever forward to lower the elevator ever so slightly for a better view. That *was* a light! It was paper thin and smoky yellow—and then it was gone once more.

Could it be only a lightning bug in the shaft? I wondered. But we didn't have lightning bugs in San Diego. I'd never actually seen one.

And I wasn't seeing one now, I assured myself. The light was back. And I was getting the hang of watching it, flashing on and off.

I heard someone below ring, but I held the elevator firmly in place. Maybe, I thought, I needed to get the light directly centered in the window, like lining up a target in crosshairs. Perhaps it would position the elevator exactly between the two floors. Maybe that was the secret.

I nudged the elevator, waiting for the light streak to return, and then gently nudged a little more.

I had it centered. A brass band was blaring in my ears.

I held my breath and opened the elevator door.

The solid wall was gone.

I had found the thirteenth floor!

I rushed forward into a windy, howling blackness. The elevator clanged shut after me and dropped away.

A split second later I felt the floor heave up under me. I was pitched like a kicked cat into the wall at my left. Earthquake! I thought. I reached out my hands to steady myself. I was smelling a powerful salty wind. And then the flash of light returned, a square lantern with a flickering candle inside swinging from the ceiling of a nearby room.

From the lights and shadows being flung about the room I saw now that it wasn't an earthquake that had struck me. I had found the thirteenth floor, and it was a ship at sea.

CHAPTER 4

Captain Crackstone

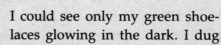

I could see only my green shoe-laces glowing in the dark. I dug the pencil flashlight out of my backpack, but put it away once I reached the lantern in the next room. I unhooked the thing from the rough wooden beam overhead. I looked all around but could see nothing but the damp planks under my feet and the wet, glistening ribs of the ship itself. I felt as if I'd been swallowed by a whale.

I was able to anticipate the next roll of the sea and steadied myself. I could hear a sloshing below my feet, like water in a dishpan, from one side of the ship to the other.

I'd heard of foul bilgewater that collected in the bottoms of ships, and I supposed that's what it was. It smelled worse than dead rats. There seemed an awful lot of sloshing going on. With fresh alarm, I raised the lantern to what appeared to be a fine leak shooting out like steam from the ship's ribs. Wasn't there anyone aboard this ship to fix leaks?

As I stumbled forward, I knew by the rough bunks along the walls that I was in the crew's quarters. And I realized for the first time that the radio at my ears had gone dead. I pulled it down around my neck.

Where was the crew? There must be someone aboard. The candle in the lantern I was holding couldn't have lit itself.

And then, with a sharp heave of the ship, the lantern was knocked from my hand and the candle was snuffed out. My green shoelaces glowed up again, but they hardly gave off as much light as cat's eyes. In the deep blackness I began feeling my way like a blind man without a stick.

"Liz?"

She must be somewhere aboard this ship. I was anxious to find her and let her see that I had found the thirteenth floor, too.

I don't know where the hand came from, but as suddenly as a stab of lightning it clamped my shoulder.

"Save me wretched soul!" shouted the man, his breath at my ear. "It's a ghost crawling up from the bilge! An unholy spirit!"

"No, sir—"

"Aye, ye forgot to turn the ghostie lights off yur feet, didn't ye?"

"These are only glow-in-the-dark shoelaces!" I said. "I'm not a ghost!"

He shoved me roughly forward. "On deck! And don't try any spirit tricks or the captain'll fling yur wispy hide overboard! Afraid of nothing is the captain! Drowns hobgoblins as easy as a sackful of cats, I wouldn't be surprised."

We rose up a narrow stairway and came out into a dimly lit storage room. For the first time I got a look at the man urging me along. His hair and beard were such a thick tangle that there barely seemed room for his eyes to peer out and his nose to poke out. "Up! Up, ghostie!" he commanded.

For all his bold and blustering front he was clearly afraid of me, I thought. Still, his hand clung to my shoulder like a huge, hairy crab. Up we went.

When we came out on the deck, I could hardly tell whether it was day or night. The ship was tossing about in a screeching black storm. Gale winds almost snatched the air out of my mouth. A wave crashed over the deck and might have washed me away, except for the sailor's iron grip. He'd caught a goblin, and he wasn't going to let go. He gave me a shove toward the rear of the ship.

I saw now that this was an old sailing ship. In flashes of lightning I made out the crew up among the glistening ropes as they struggled to lower canvas against the storm.

As we reached the rear of the ship, the ghost catcher shouted in my ear. "Up the ladder! To the quarterdeck, and mind yur manners!"

I recognized the quarterdeck from movies I'd seen. It rose like a stage where the ship's captain would strut about and shout orders. But if that was the captain suddenly exposed in a flare of lightning, he was neither strutting nor shouting. A black cloak billowed from his shoulders.

He stood calmly, peering at the barefoot sailors moving like tightrope walkers overhead.

"Look what I found!" shouted the bearded sailor, glad to be turning his prize loose at last. "Climbin' up out of the bilge, he was! And us who ain't touched land in three months. What could it be but a Madagascar ghost prowling about, sir? A genuine haunt! Aye, his feet is still aglow! Shall I kick it overboard?"

The captain's cloak snapped and cracked like a dark flag. "I think not, sailmaker," he said airily. "Ghosts can swim like herrings, my good fellow. Leave the intruder to me. Say no more about it—not a word, sailmaker, not a whisper. If I hear any mutterings about ghosts, I'll toss *you* overboard. Now be so kind as to lend a hand at the mainmast brace."

"Aye, sir. Swim like herrings, do they?"

"Not a word!"

The sailmaker scrambled down the ladder, and the captain turned his full and burning gaze upon me. Against the black storm he stood bareheaded, with his longish hair flying about his face. He didn't look exactly overjoyed to see me aboard.

"What nature of fool are you?" he shouted. His voice was as English around the edges as Abigail Parson's. He sounded like one of the Beatles, without the guitars. "Have you no better sense than to pass yourself off as a ghost among superstitious sailors? What are you wearing on your toes?"

"It's just my shoelaces, sir!"

"Shoelaces? What in creation are they?"

I peered hard up into his eyes. He must know what shoelaces were!

"You could Jonah our voyage home!" he continued. "Doom us! The crew will be trying to chase you off with blades and hot pokers!"

"I didn't know I'd be mistaken for a ghost, sir!"

"How did you get aboard?" he roared. "Is the Red Sea pirate still trailing us, eh? Were you swept off her like a chip of wood in the storm? Did you hoist yourself aboard us? Speak up!"

"No, sir. I stepped out of the elevator and—"

"Elevator! What's that?"

"Sir?" I stared at him, all dressed up in a red coat and flying black cape as if he'd come from a costume party. I was getting a creepy feeling about this weathered old ship and its barefoot crew.

"Swallowed your tongue, have you?" he snapped impatiently. "Declare yourself! What nature of off-ox English is it you speak? And this ods bodkins costume you're wearing? How'd you turn up aboard, eh? Captain John Crackstone is speaking to you, lad! Answer me!"

Crackstone! The family pirate? I froze even as a blast of spray stung us like birdshot. What had I stepped into on the thirteenth floor? A jumble of thoughts swirled around my head, and I felt my breath snatched away. Hadn't Liz said that Captain Crackstone was strung up three hundred years ago? But there he stood, big as life! And here I stood, talking to him. He didn't know about elevators and shoelaces, of course! They hadn't been invented yet. If this was Captain John Crackstone, I was on a pirate ship tossed up in a storm centuries ago. I must have stumbled so far back in time that the United States of America wouldn't even be on his map.

"Speak up!" he bellowed.

"I'm a stowaway," I burst out. He'd take me for a lunatic if I tried to explain about tall buildings and thirteenth floors.

"A stowaway!" he shouted, as if a keg of gunpowder had blown up under him "Don't you know a captain would as soon have sea worms as a food-pilfering stowaway aboard!"

"I'm sorry, sir," I answered. "But I've run off to sea."

"Have you! In the middle of the infernal ocean!"

"No, sir." I went racing through my head for an answer that might make sense when he answered for me.

"I suppose you crept aboard as my sailmaker reasoned—at pestiferous Madagascar!"

I leaped at this possibility. "That's it, sir. Pestiferous Madagascar." I'd forgotten exactly where Madagascar was, but it sounded reasonable to me. "And my sister came aboard with me. You must have her safe in one of the cabins, sir."

"Bold as brass, you are!" and I saw his teeth flash in a passing smile. "Ods-bob, am I to believe, lad, that you've kept yourself hidden and fed since Madagascar—with none of my crew sniffing you out? You who after three months in the bilge would smell higher than a hogshead of rotten fish?"

I changed the subject. "Sir, with the storm and all, I'm sorry to bring you bad news, but you've got a leak in the bottom of your ship."

"Only one?" he replied. He didn't alarm easily. "How big a leak?"

"Like a crack in a garden hose."

"A what?" His eyes narrowed, and I realized that again he didn't know what I was talking about.

"Just a leak, sir," I answered quickly.

"Mr. Dashaway," he called out, turning to a giant with a squashed nose and big buckles on his shoes. "Sir, this stowaway tells me there's a leak in the bilge. See to it in your leisure. If we begin to sink, you may see to it in haste."

"A stowaway, Captain?"

"Hidden as cleverly as a flea."

I'm not sure Captain Crackstone believed my story. But

I think he chose to have a stowaway aboard rather than a ghost to rattle the crew and Jonah the voyage home. A Jonah, I figured, must mean the worst kind of bad luck.

He turned back to me. "I keep no guests aboard. You'll turn to on deck until we reach port."

"Yes, sir."

Until that moment I hadn't noticed that he carried a copper speaking trumpet under his arm. He now lifted it to his lips and called out below to a little man with a yellow scarf tight and wet around his head.

"Bosun! The mainstays are singing a better tune! This squall is playing itself out. We'll have sunshine for supper, I promise you!"

I felt hypnotized by the glistening copper trumpet. How new it looked, without a dent in it, but how familiar! At this same moment it must be standing on the bookcase in my dad's room at home.

"Bosun!"

"Aye, sir!"

"Any glimpse of the Red Sea rascal?" shouted Captain Crackstone.

"None, sir!"

"Those cutthroats can smell treasure across a thousand leagues of sea!"

"Worse'n dogs for it!"

So there was treasure aboard! And I might be here to catch sight of them burying it!

Again shouting into the trumpet, Captain Crackstone said, "Post a lookout as soon as the sea behaves itself!"

"My men ain't had a wink o' sleep."

"I'll send you a lookout," he called, and turned to me. "You won't mind accommodating us by taking up lodgings in the crow's nest, will you, lad? Soon as we can see beyond our own figurehead.''

I had an idea what the crow's nest was. It must be the barrel I saw way up at the top of the mast. I peered at it now, whipping back and forth with the ship, like the metronome on our piano at home. Anyone climbing to the crow's nest could be flung right out again. It looked scary.

''Yes, sir, I can hardly wait to climb up there,'' I said. ''But I'd rather stay alive.''

''Why, lad, at the age of nine I was scampering up the ratlines, those rope ladders there,'' he answered. ''Scrambling up to the crow's nest is a splendid way to learn the sailoring profession.''

I was sorry now that I'd said I had run away to sea. ''The truth is, I only came aboard to look for my sister.''

He gave me a sharply curious look. ''Your sister?''

''Yes, sir.''

''Are you daft? We carry no women aboard.''

''But she must be here! Somewhere!''

''And I tell you that she is not.''

I tried not to let my thoughts panic. Of course she was here. Finding herself among pirates, Liz must be keeping herself hidden. I'd find her.

CHAPTER 5

The Laughing Mermaid

 Behind me a door was banging. "Wait in the chart house there!" he told me. "And secure that door before the wind pulls it off by the hinges!"

I wasn't sorry to get out of the weather. The chart house was a polished wooden box of a room with a low ceiling. Hanging from an iron hook, a lantern was screeching like a stepped-on cat with every roll of the ship.

I quickly pulled out my shoelaces before someone else could mistake me for a ghost. Then I stood gazing around. Water rolled down my arms and off my backpack, as if I had just stepped out of a shower. A shower? These men aboard wouldn't know what I was talking about.

Behind the table stood a large chair, and I was disappointed not to see Liz sitting there and smiling at me. But of course, she wouldn't be out in the open if she was hiding.

I gathered up a large map blown to the floor and had a look. I found Boston easily enough, and I guessed a pen-and-ink line approaching the coast must be the ship's route. We appeared to be just past an island marked Nantucket. And there was the name of the ship:

VOYAGE OF
The Laughing Mermaid
P R I V A T E E R
In the Years 1691 & 1692

I wasn't sure what a privateer was, but I supposed it was some brand of pirate. I traced the ship's voyage backward across the Atlantic Ocean and around the tip of Africa and up the far coast to a huge island, Madagascar. So that's where I said I'd come aboard! The route continued north to a narrow strip of water marked "Red Sea." There the ship's route was scribbled back and forth, like earthquake scratchings on the Richter scale. Maybe that was where the *Laughing Mermaid* had done her plundering.

"Liz?"

I had unhooked the lantern and now called down a narrow stairway. There were cabins below, including a long room with a table and chairs that looked as if it might be the place the captain and his officers lived.

"Liz?"

I must have stumbled into the captain's cabin, for it was kind of grand with windows that ran across the entire back of the ship. Sea-foam kept blowing up to the glass, hanging there like lace until the next wave washed things away. I paused before an oil painting of a dark-eyed woman who appeared to be on the verge of smiling and a boy about my own age. He was all dressed up in a big starched collar and looked uncomfortable about it. I suppose they were the captain's family.

"Stowaway!"

I turned to to see hovering over me the huge man with the squashed nose, Mr. Dashaway.

"Thievin' the captain's quarters, are ye?" he shouted.

"No, sir! I think there's another stowaway aboard, and I was looking for her. My sister. You must have seen her!"

"The only female I've seen is braced to the bow."

"Braced?"

"The figurehead, boy. The mermaid! Have you never seen a ship in your life?"

"Not a sailing ship," I answered.

He shook his head in wild disbelief. "Like saying you've never seen a bird in the air, *that* is!" he scoffed. "Not only a stowaway and a thief but a liar in the bargain."

"I haven't stolen anything!"

"The captain'll judge that for himself. Now, where is it you discovered a new leak? Show me!"

He took the lantern out of my hand and led me down from deck to deck. I could hear the sea pound like a huge drum against the hull. At the same time I had a faint sense that the ship was not crashing about as wildly as before. My eyes kept darting to the shadows for a glimpse of Liz. Where was she?

Once we were down to bilgewater, we could see another lantern swinging about.

It was Captain Crackstone, who must have come to look for himself. I was sure now that the storm was weakening if Captain Crackstone felt able to leave his quarterdeck.

"Lead the way," he said to me.

We crept farther toward the rear of the ship. Liz wouldn't be hanging around in this foul-smelling bilge, I told myself—not without a clothespin on her nose.

I pointed to the leak. "There, sir."

Captain Crackstone squinted an eye and gave out a small chuckle. "Why, lad, that's hardly more than a pinprick, wouldn't you say, Mr. Dashaway?"

Mr. Dashaway turned out to be the first mate, next in command to the captain himself. He rubbed his squashed nose and in a voice full of gravel declared, "That pinprick'll sink us, Captain. It's going to burst open like a boil."

"Now, sir, you do take a dark view of the world."

"And you don't take it serious, Captain. We need to careen the ship and scrape 'er bottom and plug 'er up."

"I believe it can wait until we reach Boston. I haven't seen my wife and son in two years!"

"And if we sink, you won't see them for an eternity," said the first mate. "Cast your eyes at the quantity of water slopping about the bilge. The hull's leaking like a basket, and us with both our pumps crushed to matchsticks! We've grown so much sea grass we can hardly make headway. I say we change course and beach the ship, sir!"

"And I say, straight on to Boston, Mr. Dashaway. Now we've taken in our top laundry"—I guessed he meant the topsails—"give the men an hour's rest. Then call all hands to bail out this bilgewater. We'll mop it up dry as parchment and fix what we can with copper flashing. We've sheets of it still, haven't we?"

I gazed into the wet blackness. Somewhere beyond the range of the lantern lay the thirteenth floor. I could dodge out of here in seconds. But no, not without Liz. And what about the treasure? Was that what filled the chests and boxes I'd already noticed in the captain's cabin and below-decks?

Mr. Dashaway started away. Then he stopped to eye me in the lantern light. "I found that scrawny rascal prowlin' your cabin, Captain. And lyin' his head off. Says he never saw a ship before, and him at sea!"

"I'll take care of it, Mr. Dashaway."

"I wasn't lying," I said softly. "I was prowling, but I wasn't stealing!"

"We shall see."

He held the lantern and led the way back to his cabin. "What sea name do you call yourself by?"

"Stebbins," I said.

He swung about. "Are you trying to mock me?"

"No, sir. My name is Stebbins."

He raised the yellow light to my eyes. "Stebbins," he repeated like a sharp echo.

"Same as you," I said boldly.

By now his nose was practically in my face. "Stebbins is my name? Who put such a mad notion in your head?

"I read it."

"The lad can read. And in the London broadsides, I suppose! Where is it written that Pirate John Crackstone and Captain John Stebbins are one and the same?"

"Around and about," I answered vaguely.

"So my secret is out."

I could also inform him that he'd be going to the gallows for piracy, but I decided it wouldn't be courteous. And I wasn't going to tell him that he was a distant ancestor of mine. He'd regard me as a lunatic. "You're bound to be famous, sir!"

"Famous?" he muttered. "Famous? That is bad news for a gentleman in my profession." And then he chose to regard the matter with a flashing smile. "Is there a price on my head?"

"I wouldn't be surprised, sir."

"I shall double it!" he said, laughing, and dismissed the matter. Again he asked, "What out-of-tune English is it that you speak? What colony bred you up?"

I wasn't sure that California was yet on his maps, so I said, "West of Boston, sir."

"Vermont, perhaps?"

"Farther west than that," I said. A lot farther.

He shrugged and let it go. "It's your business."

Once we reached his cabin, he hung the lantern from a ceiling hook, and he took a quick glance around.

"I didn't take a thing, sir," I said. "You can look in my bag."

"That won't be necessary, Stebbins. I see nothing missing."

"Please look!" I said, anxious to be clear of any suspicion. "Just a few schoolbooks, mostly."

I emptied everything on the floor, which was still heaving about, but not enough to knock you off your feet. I hoped he wouldn't ask about my pencil flashlight or mini tape recorder. It would take me ten years to explain.

"Aye, I took you for a scholar," he said. He fished out one of the books, my history book, and split it open. He held it closer to the lantern, turned the page, and smacked his lips. "What's World War Two, Stebbins?"

"It's kind of hard to explain."

"Dragonflies?"

His finger was on a picture of airplanes in a dogfight over France.

"Yes, sir," I said.

He flipped the pages and stopped. "What a fantastical doll."

The Statue of Liberty. "Right," I said.

He snapped the book shut. "Schoolboy rubbish."

"Of course. You can see I'm not hiding anything."

He stripped off his wet cloak. "Stebbins, not even a numskull would snatch anything but a crust of bread in the middle of the sea. Where would you run and hide the spoils, eh?"

"Your treasure's safe from me, sir," I said. "I'm only looking for my sister."

He gave me a sharper look. "Who was babbling about treasure aboard?"

"You, sir."

He paced along the row of windows and then ripped out a laugh. "Babbling, was I? Well, well. But did I say where the plunder's hid? I think not! I don't leave treasure lying about for any whipjack to fancy. The plunder's aboard, young Stebbins, but not even my crew knows where I keep it snugged. It makes them marvelous loyal, lad. Aye, and they'll keep this treasure ship afloat if they have to swim on their backs and hold it up!"

"Are they cutthroats?" I muttered.

"Only half of them. The other half are murderers." He fell, laughing, into a large velvet chair behind the chart table. "At sea, lad, we don't inquire too closely into a man's past. We're a privateer, you see, with a charter from the king himself to prey on his enemy's ships. Fortunately he's rich in enemies! Are we still at war with France?"

"I wouldn't know, sir,"

"Well, look you, it's not true we attacked an English ship with the Red Sea treasure in its hold. She was flying no flag at all! Beached and bleached like a dead whale in the Red Sea sand. The king may claim the treasure, but he'll have to hang me first. I intend to share out with my crew once we drop the hook in Boston Harbor."

I could have told him that yes, the king was going to hang him. But he wouldn't believe me. How could I know a terrible thing like that? I said nothing.

"Now dry your clothes at the galley stove," he told me. "When I want you to squirrel up the mast, I'll send for you."

CHAPTER 6

The Bloody Hand

I didn't head for the galley fire. I went poking around, again looking for Liz. Once we found each other, we could return to the thirteenth floor and I could dry out in San Diego.

Was she curled up somewhere, seasick? She couldn't have noticed that I was aboard. Even with the wind ripping about, I would have heard her call out my name.

After knocking at cabin doors, I shrugged and figured she wasn't hiding in the rear of the ship. I made my way forward. When I came to a low room with a flaming stove, I knew it must be the galley. Men who had come in from the weather now stripped off their coats to dry around the fire and stood about chattering.

"Land's so close I can smell it," I heard someone say.

"Don't count yur treasure till it's shared out, matey."

"Where do you suppose he keeps it? Under that feather mattress o' his?"

"I looked."

Keeping to the shadows, I slipped past them unseen. I ventured forward into what I took to be the forward crew's quarters. Bunks all around were piled with straw like big nests. Where the ship narrowed to cut through the sea, I made out a cargo of rolled-up carpets.

I stopped short. To my left stood the bushy-faced sailmaker. His eyes, fixed on me, glowed like red-hot coals.

"Befuddled the captain, did ye? But not me, ye didn't!" he declared in a low, rumbling voice. "I knows a sea ghost when I lays eyes on one. You dredgies rise up from the deep and climb aboard any passing ship that suits ye. Aye, how else could you turn up in the middle of the ocean, tell me? You're dredged up from the deep, that's what. Stay out of the fo'c'sle here with yur dead touch. Back off!"

I didn't try to argue with him. If he believed in sea ghosts, I could cut a finger and he wouldn't believe it was real blood. I backed off. The fo'c'sle could wait. I'd check it later.

I climbed up through a hatch and looked around. Only a short man steering the ship was left out in the weather. I saw that waves were no longer breaking over the deck. Except for the lower sails, the masts stood as bare as telephone poles.

I grabbed a railing and moved past a row of cannons to a boat lying across the deck. It was turned over, like a turtle shell, and lashed down. It would have made Liz a great shelter and a place to hide. I dropped to my knees and poked my head under the edge of the boat.

"Hey, Liz. It's me, Buddy."

But there came no answer.

I looked back at the masts and was relieved to see that they were no longer whipping madly across the sky. My gaze settled on the crow's nest. It appeared to be nothing more than an open barrel mounted to the forward mast. What a place to hide! If it had frightened Liz to find herself among pirates, she might have curled up in that barrel. The wonder of it would be if the high seas hadn't pitched her out like a slingshot.

I kept to myself for a while, but my glance kept returning to the crow's nest. You've got to be somewhere, Liz, I thought. And you're just contrary enough to be hiding away in the worst possible place. You there? Did you climb up during the night?

I didn't think she was. But I wasn't going to know if I didn't poke my head in and take a look.

My heart began to pound. The thought of climbing out over the rail and onto the rope ladder was scary. And if I thought about it a moment longer, I'd be too scared to try.

I kicked off my shoes and pulled myself onto the thick wooden rail. I grabbed the rope ladder with my hands and reached out with my left foot for a cross rope to stand on.

"Bless my eyesight!" The captain was suddenly standing hardly five feet away. "Can't wait to climb the ratlines, eh, young Stebbins? Can't wait to commence your sea learning!"

I said nothing. I just gazed down at him.

"A lookout needs to know what to look out for," he said grinning. "Kindly don't disturb me if you see the spout of a whale, Stebbins, or a pink sunset or a school of codfish. It's the *Bloody Hand* you're to clap eyes on."

"The *Bloody Hand*?" I asked.

"Aye. Such a villainous ship that not even barnacles will sail with her. The pirate scum of the Red Sea sails under her skull and crossbones! And the worst of the lot is my old shipmate Captain Harry Scratch. He smells treasure the way a shark follows fresh blood. He's tried to board us twice since we left Madagascar, and he'll try again. The *Bloody Hand* is out there in the gloom, young Stebbins. Aye, trailing us like a shark."

Suddenly he was holding out his speaking trumpet to me.

"Take this up the ratlines with you. You'll need it in the wind. If you spy the merest rag of sail, sing out! Burst your lungs!"

When I took the trumpet in my hand, it was like touching home. No doubt about it, this was the same copper megaphone I'd held to my lips in San Diego when I'd called out to Captain Crackstone.

"Up you go!" he commanded. "Secure yourself to the mast, and keep your eyes sharp."

I slipped the trumpet into my windbreaker and zipped it in tighter. Out of the corner of my eye I saw bafflement flash across Captain Crackstone's face. It took me only a second to figure out why. The zipper, of course.

I left the rail and clung like a cat to the rope ladder. Glancing down, I watched the cold sea racing and foaming below me. Shouldn't I have a life preserver? Or hadn't it been invented yet, either?

I climbed upward, hand over hand and foot over foot. I wished now I'd left off my backpack. The weight of my schoolbooks kept tugging at my back.

The ladder narrowed the higher I climbed, and the wind seemed sharper. Finally the crow's nest was within reach, and I called out, "Liz! Gimme a hand!"

She didn't. The crow's nest was empty. I felt sharply exasperated, and angry with Liz for keeping herself so scarce. Why couldn't she be like other people and just turn up?

I climbed into the crow's nest, relieved to be off the none-too-steady ratlines. I found a wet rope looped around the mast and tied it with a couple of big knots around my waist. At least I wouldn't be pitched out to sea.

I looked all around but saw no flash of sail out on the ocean. Now that we were leaving the black storm behind, a low streak of sunlight appeared under the clouds, like light under a door.

Glancing down from that height, I was surprised to see how narrow the ship looked. As the mast swayed and creaked, I found myself suspended over the sea on one side and then the other. It amazed me that I hadn't become seasick. I must have an iron stomach, I thought. Maybe I'd inherited it from Captain Crackstone himself.

I ducked into the barrel to get out of the wind for a while and fished in the backpack for my Walkman. Maybe I could get it to work again. It would pass the time to have something to listen to. But the battery had gone absolutely cold, stone dead.

But no. It couldn't be the battery. I was picking up static.

I took a breath. Dummy! *There were no stations.* Radio hadn't been invented!

I zipped my windbreaker all the way to my throat and

thought about my Spanish test. I'd missed it, of course. What excuse could I make? That I'd taken a flying leap back three hundred years? My final grade was going to be a disaster.

"All hands! All hands!"

It was Mr. Dashaway's booming voice below. Before long I saw a bucket brigade form like an ant trail through the open hatch. It must have gone down to the bilge. Moments later the end man, on deck, began tossing bucket after bucket of water back into the sea.

I watched with a feeling that maybe I'd saved the ship from sinking. What if no one had noticed that leak? As Mr. Dashaway himself said, it could burst open like a boil.

The pirates below spent hours trying to dry out the bilge, and still the buckets kept coming. I didn't want to let Captain Crackstone down and allow the *Bloody Hand* to sneak up on him, so I kept a sharp eye on the waters around us.

The wind died away, but the streaky daylight didn't last long. Fog began drifting by like torn rags floating in the air. Soon we went plowing into a solid bank of fog. Bilgewater kept rising, bucket by bucket, out the hatch and over the side.

I figured the captain wouldn't need a lookout in the fog. But shouldn't I wait for an order? Soon I could hardly see a ship's length in any direction.

Had the captain forgotten I was up in the crow's nest? After a while I untied the rope around my stomach. It was dumb to stay up on the mast.

That's when I saw the flash of sail.

A ship came bursting out of the mist. It bore down to

the left of us. The painted figurehead dipped into a wave and then rose, dripping seawater.

It was the carved figure of a pirate in a flowing blue coat. He was holding up a wounded right hand, dripping blood.

The *Bloody Hand*!

CHAPTER 7

Captain Scratch

I was so startled that for a moment I couldn't find my voice. I saw a couple of grappling hooks fly through the air and catch like claws on our railings. At the same time pirates began to swing on ropes to board us.

I jammed the speaking trumpet to my teeth.

"The *Bloody Hand*!" I yelled. "Captain! Captain! They're coming aboard! The *Bloody Hand*!"

Swinging on their ropes, the pirates dropped aboard like a hatching of spiders. But hardly a soul remained on deck to fight them off. There was only the sailor with the bilge bucket and the steersman at his great wheel, and the pirates had them at sword's points in an instant.

Then the men of the *Bloody Hand* slid the hatches shut, locking the crew belowdecks. At the same moment Captain Crackstone came bursting out of the chart house.

He was flashing a cutlass in one hand and a knife in the other. He leaped down the stairs and into the invaders.

In the gloomy light I could see sparks fly as the blades met and clashed. He was far outnumbered! I expected to see him cut down before my eyes, and I held my breath. But he kept charging one and all, yelling insults as he went.

"Snorting cockroaches! Off my ship, you potbellied muckworms!"

With the grappling hooks in place, the two ships were now drawn side by side. Pirates of the *Bloody Hand* continued spilling over the rails of the *Laughing Mermaid*.

Captain Crackstone was now forced to back up. He flung the dagger, taking off a pirate's hat. In the next instant I saw him leap to the ratlines.

Facing outward, he continued swinging his cutlass. But a moment later the pirates were on the ratlines, too, forcing him higher.

Rung by rung he backed up the ladder toward me. And rung by rung the pirates pursued him.

Suddenly there came a booming voice from the *Bloody Hand*. I saw a big man standing with his legs apart and a curly bear's hide thrown across his shoulders. His beard was so red and wild it looked like a bonfire.

"Gads so! If it ain't the gentleman pirate and me old shipmate John Stebbins, fightin' for his life again."

"Harry Scratch, where did you find these puny sea maggots? I've fought off flies that annoyed me more."

"They'll do, John. I can smell the Red Sea treasure aboard, and I mean to take it."

"Red Sea treasure? Sea gossip! You won't find ducats and doubloons in our hold."

"Ducats and doubloons!" Captain Scratch scoffed. "Common as buttons, John! It was you who fell like a vulture on the Great Mogul's shipwrecked treasure! Aye, with diamonds and rubies and emeralds to rival sparkling sunlight itself! Surrender, John!"

"Go to splintered lightning!" yelled Captain Crackstone.

The puny sea maggots kept backing him higher and higher toward the crow's nest. They looked far from puny to me. He must know he was facing certain death.

Captain Scratch ripped out a laugh. "We got ye trapped like a spider in yer own web, John!"

"Search the *Laughing Mermaid* from bowsprit to rudder," shouted Captain Crackstone, "and the only diamond you'll find is on a pack of cards."

"Hackle me bones, that would disappoint me terrible, John. I'll take yer ship apart timber by timber if I have to, and over yer dead body if ye press me to it. Stop yer snappin' that cutlass like the tail of a stingray and I'll give ye quarter. I swear on me oath as a thief and a murderer to spare yer life, John. Aye, I'll put ye aboard yer ship's boat and wish ye luck."

"And my crew? Every man spared?"

"Ye drive a hard bargain, John! Aye, I'll spare the crew, every man."

Captain Crackstone sheathed his cutlass with a loud clack. "Harry Scratch, lower away the boat!"

The big pirate swung aboard and began shouting orders. "Gallows Bird! Billy Bombay! Fetch a keg of water for me old shipmate, and a ration or two of sea biscuits, if you can find any. Lower the boat!"

It wasn't long before the boat was over the side and ready for sea. One by one the crew of the *Laughing Mermaid* was let up out of the hatch and disarmed.

I began the climb down from the crow's nest. I intended to return the speaking trumpet, for I knew it was destined to find its own way to San Diego. But I had no intention of joining Captain Crackstone in the small boat. I couldn't leave Liz alone aboard the *Laughing Mermaid*. And if I left the ship, I'd never again be able to find my way back to the thirteenth floor!

Before long the crew of the *Laughing Mermaid* was rounded up, and Captain Scratch stood on the hatch cover to make a speech.

"Look ye, mates! Go with yer captain or stay aboard and join as fine a company of full-rigged cutthroats as ever was born! What's yer choice?"

I was amazed to see not a man step forward to join Captain Crackstone.

"Oho, John!" Captain Scratch coughed up a laugh. "There's proof of a cargo of treasure aboard! Aye! These swine have shown their greedy colors. It ain't you that commands their loyalty, John—it's the Red Sea plunder!"

Mr. Dashaway did look a little sheepish, I thought, but Captain Crackstone ignored them all. He demanded his sea chest and compass. Captain Scratch sent the little man he called Billy Bombay to get them and then turned to a cutthroat wearing a slouchy hat with peacock feathers sticking out of it.

"Gallows Bird, I elect ye captain of this ship."

"Strike me dead!"

"I will if ye stray an inch out of my shadow. But Captain Gallows Bird has a gloomy ring to it. What's yer born name?"

The pirate seemed thrown into confusion. Maybe it was Percy or Clarence or some name that didn't quite suit a buccaneer. Finally he said, "Baptize me a new name for luck, Captain."

"Then I'll baptize you Captain Crackstone, and hope you'll have as much luck with it as John Stebbins, who won't be needing it any longer!"

By that time Billy Bombay was returning with the captain's sea chest. I slipped to deck and found my shoes. I was about to hand the captain his speaking trumpet when I saw him whispering a few clipped words to Mr. Dashaway. Mr. Dashaway gave a nod of his eyes. They were conspiring something, I thought. At the same time the sailmaker began waving his arms.

"Don't leave that one aboard!" he cried out, pointing at me. "A ghost he is. A dredgie!"

Captain Scratch's eyes flashed my way. "God preserve us all in our right wits—a dredgie?"

"I seen him with me own eyes!" The sailmaker went on. "He forgot to snuff out the lights at his feet, sir, and I seen them glowing like green moonlight. Aye—he's a sea ghostie!"

Captain Crackstone already had his legs over the side. "Sea rubbish!" he snapped. "Let the lad stay aboard. He doesn't walk through walls. He's just a boy."

Captain Scratch's fingers lost themselves in his spiky red beard. "Well, now, that may be, shipmate. But a dredgie ain't pleasant to have aboard. Makes me shiver, they do! So take him aboard yerself, John."

"Aye, let's take no chances," said Gallows Bird.

He drew his sword and prodded me over the side. I

had hardly landed in the boat when the captain shoved us away from the hull.

As I watched the ship recede, I felt as if I were drowning with my eyes wide open. My only way back home grew fainter and fainter in the mist, and then the sails of the *Laughing Mermaid* vanished completely.

CHAPTER 8

Adrift at Sea

 We drifted all night, for Captain Crackstone discovered there was no sail aboard and only one broken oar. Even worse, the keg of water thrown down to us turned out to be molasses, and we had nothing to drink.

"We'll worry about that tomorrow," the captain said, as if it were a matter hardly worth losing a wink of sleep over. He dug into his oak sea chest and tossed out a heavy coat with brass buttons and other articles of clothing. "Make your bed as best you can, Stebbins."

With his coat as a mattress, I had only a little trouble falling asleep. I was tired enough, but I kept thinking of the *Laughing Mermaid* sailing off, and the thirteenth floor with her. Liz could duck back home anytime she wanted to, and maybe she already had. Perhaps that was why I could never find her.

But what about me? If I didn't perish at sea, I'd be trapped in the seventeenth century, like Captain Crackstone himself.

* * *

"Rise up and shine, lad!" It was hardly dawn, and Captain Crackstone needed the coat I was sleeping on.

I woke up thirsty but swallowed a couple of times and tried to put the matter out of my mind. I trailed a hand over the side and scooped up a handful of seawater to rinse my face.

"Don't drink any of that," the captain warned. "Seawater'll drive you madder'n squirrels."

The sun bobbed up like a cork on the horizon. The captain threw back the lid of his sea chest and dug out a needle as large as a bent nail. Peering down his sharp nose, he began stitching his clothes together.

I studied him for a long time, wondering if he'd been drinking seawater. He was sewing a white shirt to the tail of his coat. Had squirrels begun running around in his head?

"We'll rig us a sail," he said, as if he could read my mind. "What's that fanciful bangle on your wrist, Stebbins?"

Before pausing to think, I answered, "My wristwatch."

"A talisman for luck, is it?"

I just nodded and let it go at that. How could I explain it was a thing that told time and was also a stopwatch and had a calculator built in? And that it cost only $4.95 on sale? He might not even know what dollars were.

After a while he showed me how to use the needle. It was shaped like a cat's claw; a sailmaker's needle, he said it was. I sewed a nightshirt with large stitches to one side of the coat. The captain took his cutlass and shaved the broken oar down so that it fitted into the hole for the missing mast.

"Hungry?" he asked. "Starved, eh?"

I nodded, and he went rummaging around for the sea biscuits. There weren't any. Food for the voyage had been forgotten. I heard Captain Crackstone mutter an oath, but I saw he wasn't one to linger over disappointments. A moment later he took a couple of writing quills from his chest. After cutting off the ends, he handed one to me. "Suck out a little of the molasses. Only a very little, hear? Make the taste linger, lad. Enjoy every drop as if it was a leg o' mutton! I judge the cask to be less than a quarter full. It must last until we reach shore."

That's how we had breakfast, sucking on goose quill straws. I had a feeling that he'd been cast adrift before and knew exactly how to make the best of the worst of things.

After two or three minutes for breakfast he pounded the cork back in place, and I knew that would be the last food we'd have until noon. I was still starved.

I returned to the sailmaker's needle while Captain Crackstone took up a couple of floorboards. He used the wood to make arms for the mast.

By midmorning we had got the sail raised on the arms— yardarms, as he called them—and almost at once the patchwork sail rattled with the wind. He tied down the corners, and the sail swelled out. He jumped, chuckling, to the tiller at the rear of the boat. And off we went!

He pointed to the west. "Land, Stebbins, is somewhere yonder. A blind cat couldn't miss it. Take the helm and steer!"

I was smiling, too. Now that we were moving, I felt that we were already practically saved. And then it occurred to me that it was *impossible* for us to dry up like a pair of scarecrows and perish at sea. I knew the captain's fortune. He'd survive, and I'd survive with him, because he had a date with the hangman!

I wished suddenly that I didn't know about the gallows

waiting for him. When I saw a smile come into his eyes, all blue and sun-wrinkled, I so dreaded the thought of the hangman's rope tugging at his neck that I had to turn my own eyes away.

He showed me how to manage the tiller and busied himself taking apart his sea chest. Choosing the best pieces of oak, he carved an oar with the cutlass, and then a second one.

"The first rule of the sea, young Stebbins, is that the wind makes you no promises, except one. It'll change."

And change it did. By early afternoon the sails had slackened and fallen dead. We began to row.

"I'm sorry about your treasure," I remarked.

He gave his broad shoulders a shake. "Does one ever own a treasure?" he said. "No, lad. We may have the loan of it temporary, you might say. Aye, put it in our pockets and take it out and gaze at the pretty sparkles. But it's like saying we own the air we breathe, eh? Lad, was there ever a pocket that didn't have holes in it?"

"Where do you suppose Captain Scratch will make off to with the chests?"

His eyes flashed with contempt. "That seagoing oaf! It would wound my soul to see pearls cast before such swine! No, Harry Scratch won't clap eyes on the plunder! It's chests he'll be looking for, but chests he won't find. Let him take the silk cloths and the Turkey carpets! The Grand Mogul's brightest jewels will be looking at him, but he won't see 'em."

"Who's the Grand Mogul?" I asked, my throat now dry and raspy.

"The king of India, you might say, who stole the jewels himself, I daresay. They once rattled in the pockets of the

Great Khan himself, according to the tales. And I'll chase Harry Scratch back to the Red Sea, if I have to, to get them rattling in my pockets."

"You're going back to sea?"

"Soon as I can find a ship to sail in. A faster ship than the *Laughing Mermaid* won't be hard to find. Slowed down by the sea grass growing to her hull, the *Mermaid* is."

"Take me with you!" I blurted out.

"You? A pesky little stowaway?"

"I won't be in your way."

"You won't be in my way if I drop you ashore. But can you keep your tongue from wagging secrets, eh? That's the question. I may choose to pitch you over the side and let you drown. Aye, that would silence your tongue handsomely, would it not?"

"Handsomely and forever," I said. "But it would be easier on your conscience to take me along."

"What conscience? I'm a pirate!"

"You're a gentleman. Even Captain Scratch said so."

"Aye. It was a terrible curse laid on me."

"You'll take me along? And teach me the sea?"

"I'll teach you to hold your tongue. While we're ashore, can I trust you to remember to forget my sea name?"

"You're Captain John Stebbins."

"Then if it's the sea you want to apprentice yourself to, I'll take you along."

I felt myself break into a great smile of relief. He could go cruising for treasure. I'd go cruising for the thirteenth floor. Once aboard the *Laughing Mermaid*, I'd vanish as quick as a snap of the fingers.

But I'd be sorry to leave him. Outside of Liz he was the only family I could talk to.

We caught a fresh wind around nightfall and could rest our arms at last. With the sail again puffing out, the captain estimated our speed at three or four knots. I wasn't sure exactly how much a knot was, but I knew it must be something like a mile. He took the sextant out of what remained of his sea chest, and after some calculations he shoved the tiller. It shifted the nose of the boat somewhat more to the north.

By then we had almost stopped talking. I felt as if I'd been eating cotton, and he must have been just as dry and thirsty.

He woke me in the middle of the night.

"Stebbins," he said with obvious delight, "kindly sleep with your mouth open."

A light rain was falling!

I opened my mouth. I swallowed and opened my mouth again. In the darkness Captain Stebbins was trying to catch rainwater in his hat. But then the squall, as he called it, whisked itself away. I had hardly got a full drink out of it, but it was a mighty relief.

When the sun came out in the morning, he told me to suck at our crazy quilt of a sail. "There's a good ration of water in the hems!" he declared, tying off the tiller.

The sail felt pleasantly damp. He stationed himself at one side of the mast, and I at the other, both of us sucking the hems of his shirts before the sun dried them out.

Late that afternoon a moth, blown out to sea, appeared over the water. Its wings, lit up by the setting sun, fluttered like scraps of spotted paper.

"Are we close to land?" I blurted out.

"I wouldn't be surprised," he said.

The next morning we sailed right into Boston Harbor.

CHAPTER 9

"Arrest That Man!"

There appeared to be more ships at anchor in the bay than buildings ashore. Captain Crackstone stood squarely in the front of the boat and gazed at the city.

"Ods-bob!" he said. "How Boston has grown in two years! Wouldn't surprise me if you could count seven or eight thousand noses!"

The morning was rising sharp and clear, but a streaky dark cloud stretched over the city. He said it was only pigeons. And now that we had entered the bay, we were having to fight against a choppy sea. "It's the wind rubbing up against the ebb tide," he explained. He seemed to be taking pleasure in filling my head with the lore I'd need for a life at sea.

As we worked our way past the islands scattered about, our patchwork sail caught the attention of the ships at anchor. I could see men staring at us as if wondering what sort of driftwood the sea was washing ashore. I recognized the bright red flag of England, for it flew everywhere in the harbor and from a fort on land.

We certainly had the look of shipwreck, for by the time we reached the dock a small crowd had formed. The people were dressed mostly in black with big starchy white collars and Thanksgiving hats. Pilgrims! I thought. I felt that I had seen them before, and I had, in my schoolbooks. I gaped at them. They were real-life, living-and-breathing Puritans! It wouldn't have surprised me to see someone come along with a fan-tailed turkey.

"God bless my eyesight!" Captain Crackstone shouted. "There's my dear wife, Mercy! Mercy herself!"

I saw a tall woman in a white bonnet trying to edge her way through the crowd. Suddenly her eyes went huge and lit up, and I heard her call out, "My beloved husband!"

The captain leaped up the wharf stairs. They fell into each other's arms, and he kissed her loud.

The crowd seemed to catch its breath in sudden horror and went silent. Smiles vanished, and jaws dropped. Something had happened, but what? A heavy flight of pigeons blotted out the sun and threw a whirring shadow over the wharf.

And then I saw him, a thin man in a long black cloak and buckle shoes. He was raising his arm and pointing his finger like a signpost. "Constable!" he roared. "Arrest that man!"

My heart thumped. I thought he must have recognized John Stebbins as a pirate. Maybe there was a price on Captain Crackstone's head after all.

I saw the captain's face turn neon red. He seemed to recognize the man in black. "Arrest me! Why, sir? For what, Judge?"

"For breaking the Sabbath! Everyone here on the Town Dock witnessed it."

"What are you talking about?"

"Did you not kiss your wife on *Sunday*, Captain Stebbins?"

"After two years at sea! Indeed, I kissed my wife."

"You know the Sabbath laws of Massachusetts, Captain!"

"You expect me to know the day of the week, sir? At sea and adrift?"

"The law is the law, sir. You shall be tried and punished."

At that point Mrs. Stebbins lifted her chin and said, "Then punish me as well, Justice Rattle, for did you not see me kiss my husband?"

The man raised his pointed finger once more. "Constable, arrest them both," he declared. "I shall sentence them in the morning before the witch's trial."

I saw the captain reach for his cutlass, but Mrs. Stebbins restrained him. Two men in scarlet coats leaped alongside and grabbed his arms.

Justice Rattle flailed an arm at the crowd. "Why are you idling about? Out of my way!"

I followed as Captain Stebbins and his wife were led off to a narrow street marked Prison Lane. I drew curious glances from everyone along the way. I must have looked like a creature from outer space with my blue jeans and tennis shoes. All the men I saw wore short pants that buckled at the knees and long, baggy stockings. The boys were dressed exactly like the men. I had the feeling I was wearing the only pair of long pants in New England; maybe they hadn't been invented yet.

"And Tobias," I heard the captain say. "Where's my little son?"

Mrs. Stebbins flashed him a smile. "Little? He's growing fast, John! Off to sea, Tobias is, as cabin boy aboard the *Salem Trader*. I wouldn't be surprised if he returns an admiral."

Tobias must have reminded the captain of me, for at that moment he introduced me to his wife.

"Stebbins?" she asked. "A relative, are you?"

I said nothing.

The House of Bondage, as they called the jail, was a half-lit, drafty place. It wouldn't have surprised me to see Captain Stebbins throw off the constables and bolt the place. But I didn't think he'd leave his wife behind.

"Young Stebbins," he said to me as he was locked in with the men, "our pursuit of the *Laughing Mermaid* will be briefly delayed. You must run to the Silvernail brothers, at the sign of the Blue Barnacle, on Dock Square. Tell them to come at once!"

As his wife was parted from him and locked up with the women, she turned to me. "Cabin boy, you must then run to our home and fetch the captain a hearty meal! Had I only known he was coming! You'll find cider and gingerbread and bear sausage and dried pumpkin I stewed yesterday. Eat hearty yourself, young Stebbins!"

"Yes, ma'am," I said, feeling hungry enough to eat the bear itself, fur and all. She told me the address, and I asked for the key.

"Are you fresh from lawless London, boy? There's hardly a locked door in New England. Be off with you, young Stebbins!"

When I found the sign of the Blue Barnacle, Ship's Agents, the building looked deserted. I had to knock on all the windows before I raised one of the Silvernail brothers. He had graying hair pulled back to a short pigtail,

stuck together with what might have been tar. It gave him the look of a seaman who had grown older and prospered ashore but chose not to forget his earlier days.

He blinked his eyes sleepily and adopted a playful manner. "I'm so grateful to you, lad, for troubling to waken me," he said. "Why, I might have slept away the whole day and missed three or four splendid sermons at the meetinghouse. Can your urgent business not wait for tomorrow?"

"It can't," I said, and gave him Captain Stebbins's message.

He came fully awake and gave a shout. "Oho! Back from the sea, is John? At the prison house? I'll be there!"

He vanished from the window, and I continued on my way.

I got myself lost in one of the narrow lanes, but eventually I found the Stebbins house, sunning itself on the side of a hill. A woman stood banging on the front door. She wore a gray skirt down to the ground and a wide bonnet.

"Anybody home?" she shouted.

I would have recognized that voice anywhere. She didn't even have to turn around to face me. It was the first American voice I had heard since stepping onto the thirteenth floor.

The woman banging at the door was my sister, Liz.

CHAPTER 10

The Barn

"Buddy!" Liz shouted in a voice that shot up a couple of octaves. She gave me a smothering hug. "What are you doing here?"

And I shouted at the same moment, hugging her back. "Liz! Am I glad to see you!" At least she didn't kiss me, or we might have got arrested. "Where were you hiding? How did you get off the ship?"

"What ship?"

"The *Laughing Mermaid*. How the heck did you get here?"

"What *are* you talking about?" she exclaimed.

"I'm talking about the thirteenth floor," I replied.

And she said, "If you followed me, you must have come out into the barn. Why didn't you call out?"

I gave her a pair of crossed eyes. "What barn?"

"You know very well what barn, Buddy. The one in Northampton."

I uncrossed my eyes. "When you stepped out of the thirteenth floor, you found yourself in a barn?"

"Of course. Full of wool and cider barrels."

I felt such a surge of relief that I burst into a laugh. What did it matter if I never again laid eyes on the *Laughing Mermaid*? Liz had found a different way back to San Diego and home.

"Whose barn is it?" I asked.

"Abigail Parsons's."

"That voice on our answering machine? The woman with the Turkey shawl?"

"She's hardly a woman," said Liz. "Abigail's only ten years old."

"Where is she?"

Liz gave her left hand a toss. "Hiding in the woods over there."

"Hiding from what?"

"The sheriff. Against my best legal advice. She's due in court tomorrow."

"Ten years old," I muttered. "What did she do, jay-walk?"

Liz took a breath. "She's been accused of witchcraft."

That wiped the smile off my face. "You mean like the witchcraft stuff in Salem where they croaked a lot of people? The stuff in my history book?"

"Salem hasn't happened yet."

"You going to represent her?" I asked.

"Of course."

"Of course." I knew Liz would never be able to pass up a witch trial. And with the barn in Northampton, wherever that was, we could pop back home anytime we wanted to. I could stop worrying about the *Laughing Mermaid*.

"But first I've got to persuade Abigail to turn herself in."

"Doesn't she have any folks?"

"Her father left her in the hands of a governess while he's in England. But the governess ran off the moment Abigail was denounced as a witch. Scared stiff."

"Is witchcraft supposed to be catching or something?"

"No. But hysteria is," she said.

"Liz, you don't look like a lawyer in those threads. Have you seen yourself in a mirror? You look more like a milk-maid out of Mother Goose."

"New England isn't ready for miniskirts. This dress and apron were left behind by the governess. Abigail said I'd be arrested if I went out in the clothes I was wearing." Liz began rapping at the door again.

"There's no point in knocking, Liz. There's no one home. What are you doing here at the Stebbinses'?"

"They're Abigail's godparents. I hope they can get her to turn herself in. Buddy, what are *you* doing here?"

I explained about finding myself aboard a pirate ship and the treasure and being cast adrift with Captain Steb-bins.

"And then he was arrested for kissing his wife on Sunday!"

Liz gave a small smile and a shrug, as if quirky laws were old stuff to her.

I pushed the door open and walked into the shadowy house. "Mrs. Stebbins sent me to get Captain Stebbins something to eat. Maybe they hardly feed the prisoners in their lockup."

"Jail food is jail food."

"He's starving! Me, too." I could see the kitchen, lit up through diamond-shaped windowpanes, and found a piece of gingerbread to stuff into my mouth. I picked up a basket and filled it as fast as I could. I discovered a jug of cider and a mug that appeared to be made out of black leather.

"What if you can't get Abigail off?" I asked.

"Then she'll probably hang."

"Hang? Then what about us?"

"I'm not worried about us at the moment."

"I mean, Abigail's *got* to grow up and get married and beget children to beget descendants like us. Without Abigail what'll happen to us?"

"Maybe we'll just vanish in a couple of puffs of smoke."

"I'm serious, Liz," I said.

"Don't worry, Buddy dear. I'll get her off."

"I know another way," I said. "We take her back with us to the thirteenth floor."

Liz's eyes fluttered with a vague bafflement. "What are you talking about?"

"We go back to the barn, and presto, the three of us are back in San Diego, and she's free."

Now Liz gave me a very odd look. "It won't work."

"Sure it will."

"Buddy, there's a reason you arrived in the seventeenth century by boat."

"I believe they call it a ship."

"You couldn't have followed me into the barn."

"Why not?"

"It's the witchcraft business. Only minutes after I got to Northampton, someone torched the barn. It went up like a haystack and burned to the ground."

I exhaled. "Oh."

"I figured I'd be trapped in this skirt and bonnet forever, Buddy. I'm so relieved you found another way home."

"All Captain Stebbins has to do is find the *Laughing Mermaid*," I said. "How big is the Atlantic Ocean, sis?"

CHAPTER 11

The Girl in the Tree

I lugged the basket to the nearby woods, surrounding a kind of plaza or square with cows grazing in it. Liz said that it was called a common and that Abigail must be hiding in one of the trees.

"I can't wait around to look for her," I said.

"Abigail? Abigail!" Liz called.

"I'll be back."

Liz held her hands to her lips. "Abigail, this is my brother, Bud. I told you about him."

I saw branches rustle up in a maple tree. A thin face, white as a toadstool, peered down at me.

"Hark!" I said.

"Wake all of Boston, why don't you?" Abigail replied.

"There's no one here but the cows and us," I said.

"Don't I know it? It wouldn't surprise me if everyone's waiting at Gallows Point to see me choked off!"

"That's nonsense," Liz shouted back firmly.

"I'll run off to sea. Captain Stebbins'll see to it."

I said, "Captain Stebbins is in jail."

"In jail?" Her voice came out with a sudden wail, and I figured she was going to cry. "I'm done for!"

"Cool it," I said.

"Cool what?"

"Chill out, Abigail. I mean, calm down. When I tell the captain you're here, he'll know what to do. I'll be back as fast as I can."

I had hardly taken off when she gave a shout. "Stop your running! Don't you know it breaks the law to run on Sundays? The constables'll grab you! No hop, skip, or jumping, either!"

I walked fast.

When I reached the House of Bondage, Captain Stebbins was in heavy, whispered conversation, nose to nose, with the Silvernail brother and his tarred pigtail. Hardly more aware of me than if I were his cabin boy, the captain reached a hand out for the basket of grub and barely missed a note of their mutterings. I moved on down the hall to Mrs. Stebbins, who seemed as unconcerned and cheerful as if she were sitting in her own living room.

"Abigail charged with being a witch!" she exclaimed when I reported the news. "What wicked nonsense is this? Of course she must defend herself! I'm certain the captain will agree. You must talk that poor child down out of the tree. Tell her she's to sleep the night in our home. There are beds for all, including you yourself, young Stebbins."

On my way out I saw that the Silvernail brother was gone. Captain Stebbins's hand reached out for me and drew me to the bars of his cell.

"Tomorrow, lad," he whispered at my ear. "Stay anchored close by. I'll lay hands on a fast ship, and off we'll sail! Aye, like a bloodhound of the sea, we'll track the *Laughing Mermaid*!"

"Yes, sir," I said. I didn't see how he could trail a ship at sea with its wake now so cold, but I made myself believe that he could. Otherwise Liz and I were stuck.

When I explained about Abigail, his fingers closed angrily on the bars of the cell. "Indeed, fight the charges she must!"

When I reached the common, the cows were drinking out of the pond. Abigail was still up in the maple tree. ,

"Fight the charges I must?" she said, after I had reported my conversations. "The captain said that? And Goodwife Stebbins, too!"

"Their exact words."

"But the law'll put me in chains for dodging the sheriff! As soon as they clap eyes on me."

Liz said, "Then we'll surrender to the court tomorrow. Just before the trial."

"I'm innocent," Abigail protested. "I never rode around on a broomstick in my life!"

"Certainly not," Liz said.

"Maybe the judges'll believe me."

She started climbing down, and I started thinking about the judge who had thrown Captain Stebbins and his wife in jail. Believe Abigail? It wouldn't surprise me if he still believed the world was flat.

We spent the evening gathered around a fat yellow candle in the Stebbinses' kitchen. Liz was laying plans for Abigail's legal defense. "You say your grandmother was denounced as a witch? A spiteful neighbor getting even?"

"And declared innocent, old granny was!" Abigail answered defiantly. "But it left a stain on her. And folks think it must run in the Parsons family, being a witch, I mean. And I'm a Parsons."

"So when gossip started that there was a witch in Northampton, people immediately suspected you."

"Yes." And then she asked, "Where was it you said you came from?"

"Very far off," Liz answered. "I'll explain it more fully later."

"But I only called out to someone in my dreams. How could you hear me?"

"Somehow I did."

"And what's a Turkey shawl?" I asked.

"A shawl from Turkey, silly! Captain Stebbins brought it·back to me from one of his voyages. And he promised me a Turkey carpet."

Abigail curled up in a corner, and before long she dropped off to sleep with her mouth open.

"It's hard to imagine," I murmured, "that she's our great-great-great—great to about the fifth power—great-grandmother."

"She's darling. But she's also feisty. I hope she doesn't sound off in court and call her neighbors nitwits and jackasses."

"But what if they are? And how come they're going to hold a trial when they can't find the prisoner?"

"They'll try her anyway."

"You mean, in absentia?" I said.

Liz paused and looked at me. "Have you been reading my lawbooks?"

"Naw. You used to talk a lot at dinner. I could pass the bar."

She smiled and gave a shrug. "Yes, in absentia. From what Abigail tells me, witchcraft was too heavy for the court in Northampton, where the judge is the local brick-layer. He bumped the case up to Boston for the special court. It's meeting today. The witnesses are in town, and it'll be full steam ahead." Then she said, "I see you brought along your school stuff."

"Liz, I didn't exactly expect to turn up about twenty minutes after the *Mayflower* and miss my classes."

"What books did you bring along?"

"Math. Spanish."

"Any American history?"

I dug into my backpack. "I don't think Abigail's in it."

"The Salem witch trials will be. I hope Abigail won't be caught up in the hysteria. The judges were hanging harmless Pilgrims as witches—mostly frail old grandmoth-ers. Salem's only about twenty miles from here, and super-stition is as catching as the common cold. Do you remember the year?"

"The only dates I remember are 1492 and my birthday," I said.

She flipped the pages, gave a quick read, and glanced up. "Add 1692 to your list, Bud. That's now. And look. In a week the judges are going to hang their first witch from an oak tree—an innocent old lady named Bridget Bishop. It'll put Salem in the history books."

"They wouldn't hang a kid, would they?"

Liz gazed at Abigail and made a little shrug. "The

charges are preposterous. I ought to try an insanity defense."

"You think Abigail's nuts?"

"No. Her neighbors."

P is for
Pillory

In the middle of the night someone began rattling a drum along
the street. I turned over to go back to sleep, but I heard
Abigail jump to her feet and busy herself in the kitchen.
She began striking a flint to make a fire. As the flames
snapped and crackled, it came over me that I wasn't as
smart and clever as I thought I was. I might know how
to add and subtract on a calculator, but I had never before
worked a flint. I needed a match to start a fire.

"You could be a little more quiet out there," I called.

"Quiet? For what?" Abigail called back to me. "Didn't
you hear the watchman go by? It's four-thirty."

"You mean, the city wakes everyone up?"

"Of course. Sunday's finished, and it's Monday and
work's piled up. Go fetch us some water."

"Don't you know how to turn the faucet?"

Liz had come awake by then. "Faucet?" she said. "What
in the world's a faucet, Buddy dear? I wouldn't be surprised if you're going to have to find a pump and pump
us some water."

"It's outside," said Abigail.

That great-great-great-way-way-way-back-great-grand-mother of ours made up a big batch of oatmeal and cooked it over the fire. So what if we got trapped in the seventeenth century? I thought. We'd have fun relatives.

When I was about to leave for the jail, Abigail found a potholder and took the oatmeal off the fire. "I'll go with you," she said.

She wrapped a muffler around her nose and lips, so she wouldn't be recognized, and pulled on her bonnet. She said, "I want to see Goody and the captain before I'm carted away in chains!"

"You won't be," Liz reassured her. "Buddy, find out what time the trial is supposed to start. I want to make a few more notes."

When we reached the House of Bondage, taking turns dragging the pot of hot oatmeal, Captain Stebbins and his wife were gone. They had already been taken before Justice Rattle at the Town House for sentencing. He must have started handing out punishments at the crack of dawn.

We hurried to the Town House, a big wooden building on the corner. It rose three stories high, with a row of pillars holding the upper floors, where the court was supposed to be. But we didn't have to climb the stairs. The captain and Mrs. Stebbins were outside in plain sight.

It was as if their heads and hands had been thrust through an unpainted signboard. They had been clamped in stocks! Their punishment was to be put on display as a warning to others not to kiss on Sundays.

I decided that things were odd and crotchety in the old

days. It was okay to visit, but I hoped I wasn't going to have to live there.

I averted my eyes from Captain Stebbins. I didn't want him to notice me looking while he was being humiliated in public. But Abigail rushed forward and broke into tears.

"It's me, Abigail!" she whispered through the muffler. "What wickedness have they done you?"

Mrs. Stebbins broke into a small laugh. "A trifle, dear child! Two hours in the pillory? A fleabite compared with the joy of having my dear husband alive and fit from his voyage." She wiggled all her fingers, unable to free them from the holes in the planks. "Would you scratch the tip of my nose?"

"And drive off that pesky fly!" roared the captain.

Before long Abigail was feeding them with a spoon. I hurried up the wooden steps to the courtroom to see what time the witch trial was to start.

The room was already full of people, and there sat Justice Rattle, hammering out justice with a mallet as if he were pounding nails.

"Goodwife Marshfield, guilty of gossiping! You will wear the *G* for six months! Gossip no more!"

Down came his mallet again. "Drunk again, Mr. Tarbox? The *D* for you! Watch out that I don't brand you with an *R*, you rogue!"

Bang!

"Goodwife Fitts, wear the letter *S* and scold no more!"

I was glad to get out of there. I didn't understand the alphabet soup until I returned to the pillory and saw Mr. Silvernail and a sulky-looking man whispering to Captain Stebbins. The man was wearing a square white bib around his neck with the large black letter *R*. For *rogue*, I remembered.

But Captain Stebbins seemed not to mind. "If you know port from starboard, Mawkins, you'll do," he said. "Sign him aboard, Mr. Silvernail."

I realized then that while being clamped in the pillory, the captain was rounding up a crew. He meant to waste no time.

A moment later Liz turned up with an armful of notes, and I introduced her.

"A school-educated lawyer?" said Captain Stebbins, astonished. "Why, we'd have to sail clear to London for such a marvel! There's not a lawyer, educated or not, in all of New England."

It was Liz's turn to be astonished. "But surely the judges have their degrees," she said.

"Only degrees of ignorance, missy. Ods-bob, I doubt if any one of them has read a lawbook all the way through. The law is a trade they pick up when no one's looking."

A dismal look came over Liz. She didn't say anything, but I figured she wasn't sure how to practice law before judges who might not know any more about habeas corpus than I did.

"The trial's to start at eight-thirty," I said. "That's about twenty minutes. Sure you want Abigail to turn herself in?"

Liz lifted her chin. "Absolutely. Come on, kid. I've never lost a case yet."

That was true. But I didn't bother to say that Liz had had only a few cases.

CHAPTER 13

Pointing Fingers

Bang! went the judge's mallet, and the pigeons on the window-sill flew off. The witchcraft trial began.

, A little man with a nose like a cherry tomato turned over a large sand clock. He dipped a quill pen in ink and held it poised, ready to commit the spoken words to paper.

Justice Rattle now sat flanked by two additional judges. One was a sleepy, crumpled man with a large, heavy face, and the other was a nervous skeleton with eyes as restless as a housefly. All of them wore curly yellow wigs.

It was now standing room only in the courtroom, and as I looked around, it struck me that they all were ghosts. They had been dead in their graves for three hundred years! And yet there they stood and there they sat, whispering and nodding and coughing. In all of Boston only Liz and I were truly alive.

The mallet struck again. "Stop this rustling about," commanded Justice Rattle. He flashed his sharp profile from one side of the room to the other. "Jury, do I detect an empty chair?"

Out of breath, a burly man rushed from the door and slipped onto the chair. There were only men on the jury, and they wore their hair short and round, like wooly bicycle helmets. I noticed that I was as tall as anyone in the room, and taller than most. People must have been inches shorter in the old days, I thought. It was as if they had shrunk a size or two. I felt that I was sticking out like a flagpole and sank down as much as I could.

Abigail sat between Liz and me on a worn bench in the back. Hiding her face in the muffler, she looked ready to run for the door before it closed.

It closed.

Liz patted her hand. "The jury may be brighter than it looks," she whispered out of the side of her mouth.

"Constable, bring in the prisoner," said Justice Rattle.

There was a hurried conference, followed by a look of consternation, followed by an angry burst from the justice. "Why didn't someone tell the court before this? Is it possible that our imbecile sheriff has lost or misplaced that ten-year-old witch?"

Liz was on her feet as if shot from a cannon. "I object, Your Honor! Ten-year-old witch! Abigail Parsons has been convicted of nothing, sir! I must remind you that the witchcraft is merely alleged. She is entitled to a retraction. Perhaps the distinguished magistrate would even enter an apology."

"An apology?" The justice's gaze shot toward us like a flamethrower. "Who's addressing the court?"

"I am counsel for the defendant, sir. And Abigail Parsons is neither lost nor misplaced. She is sitting beside me and is anxious and happy to surrender to the court. Come along, Miss Parsons."

They didn't use a witness chair, so Abigail had to stand. The moment she dropped the muffler, a stocky woman jumped up in the middle of the courtroom and pointed a finger.

"That's her! That's the imp o' the devil! That's Abigail Parsons, who turned my brother into a yeller cat!"

"We don't deny she's Abigail Parsons," said Liz firmly. "I trust the balance of the woman's remarks will be stricken from the records and the minds of the jury members."

"Who . . . are . . . you?" asked Justice Rattle, taking a full and amazed breath between each word.

"Elizabeth P. Stebbins, attorney-at-law, Your Honor. As already explained, I am representing Miss Parsons in this case."

The justice exploded. "Are you mad? Women are not trained in the law! Impostor! No woman has ever appeared in my court, and never shall—except as witness or defendant!"

"And never as a member of the jury, I see," Liz answered smartly. Cool it, sis, I thought. You're here to argue witchcraft. Skip the women's rights. "One day women will be judges, I can assure you," she added, just loud enough for him to hear.

"Shall you be charged with making imbecile prophecies?" he snapped back.

"Is that against the law as well, Your Honor?"

"Sit yourself down and make no further bother! The defendant shall speak for herself. She has only to answer honestly, yes or no. She needs no counsel to speak the truth."

But Liz didn't sit herself down. "As you will not allow me to practice in your court, my associate will take over."

She raised an arm and pointed a finger directly at me. "Mr. Bud Stebbins will represent the defendant as attorney-in-fact."

I all but jumped out of my skin. Was she crazy? Just because she'd taken me to a few trials didn't qualify me to defend anyone!

For the first time the sleepy, crumpled justice seemed to come alive. He cracked the faintest of smiles.

Justice Rattle clamped his eyes on me. "He's a half-grown boy!" he exclaimed. "How old is he?"

"His age is entirely beside the point," Liz declared. "As you learned gentlemen must know, anyone may serve as *attorney-in-fact* if the accused so chooses. Anyone. Even a talking crow could serve as counsel."

The crumpled justice, whose name was Drywitt, gave out a chuckle and spoke up. "I agree, gentlemen! What an amusing situation!"

"May I advise you, sir," countered Justice Rattle, "that a case of witchcraft is not an occasion for amusement."

"In my judgment, Rattle, we cannot deny the boy."

The justices leaned their heads together to whisper and mutter. I caught Liz's arm, and we did some whispering and muttering of our own. "You gone nuts?" I said. "I can't defend Abigail! I don't know anything!"

"You want to be an actor, don't you? All you've got to do is act the part of a lawyer. Play it loose the way you did Ichabod Crane. I'll tell you what to say and do. I'll keep slipping you notes. And if I touch my chin with my thumb, just yell out 'Objection, Your Honor.' "

The three magistrates pulled their heads apart. I had a feeling that if they'd never heard of attorney-in-fact, they weren't going to admit it in public. Justice Rattle turned to Abigail.

"Accused! Do you wish to be represented by this talking boy?"

Abigail looked at Liz, who gave out a faint smile and a brisk nod.

"No question about it," declared Abigail brightly, and shifted her gaze to me. "Let him lawyer away!"

Justice Rattle irritably shuffled through some papers. Liz had won a victory, and it must have scored points with the jury. He finally pulled a document out of the pile and said, "I will now proceed to the charges."

CHAPTER 14

"Crying Out"

The courtroom had become as still as a cemetery.

"Abigail Parsons," said Justice Rattle, reading from his papers, "you are charged with suspicion of having practiced witchcraft against your neighbors. I hold in my hands four bills of indictment sent over by the grand jury of Northampton. Once, twice, thrice, four times you have been cried out as the Northhampton witch! How do you plead? Guilty?"

I saw Liz stroke her chin with her thumb, and I yelled out nervously, "Objection!"

The justice glared at me. "Objection to what?"

A wave of stage fright came over me, and I couldn't keep my hands from trembling. I managed to lean my head close to Liz and whispered, "What am I objecting to?"

"The judge's question attempts to lead the defendant. Guilty? Abigail pleads *not* guilty."

"Look at my hands," I said.

"Opening night shakes. It'll pass, Buddy dear."

I looked up and mumbled something about a leading question. Then I muttered that she was pleading not guilty.

"Let the defendant answer for herself," instructed the justice. "And in a firm voice, if you please."

Abigail spoke up in a voice that must have shaken the trees all over New England. "Not guilty! Not by a long shot!"

Justice Rattle found a piece of paper he'd been looking for, nodded, and had the first witness sworn in. It turned out to be the stocky woman who earlier had pointed her finger and called Abigail an "imp o' the devil."

"Deliverance Lankton," he said, "give us your testimony."

The woman rested her fists on her hips. "That wicked child! Certain it is she's the Northampton witch! Aye, hidin' among her good farm neighbors as if she was one of us."

Justice Drywitt bestirred himself, "This court seeks testimony, Goodwife Lankton, not opinion, no matter how charming."

"Oh, I can give you an earful of testimony!"

"Briefly."

"It happened way last year. I'd milked our cow—the brown one with the crooked tail—and set the pail down to quiet the dogs that had got into a fight, and when I carried the milk over to Jenny Gaddings, who was down sick with the ague, I met the imp o' the devil along the road—"

Liz touched her chin, and I shouted, "Objection!"

"Sustained," said Justice Rattle quickly. I guessed Liz

objected to Abigail's again being dumped on before she was convicted of anything.

The farm woman straightened her cap and went on. "It was Abigail Parsons I saw along the road, clear as I'm looking at her now, and when I delivered the milk to Jenny Gaddings, the devilment was done."

"What devilment?" asked Justice Drywitt.

"The milk soured."

"Soured?" repeated the justice.

"Quicker 'n scat. Everyone knows that if a witch glances at a pail of milk, it'll curdle."

Liz motioned me over and whispered fast, "Find out who else saw the pail of milk."

I whispered back. "It's like that case you had back home—that guy who was supposed to have the evil eye and made flowers wilt."

Liz nodded quickly. "Things change; some things never do. Could it have been the weather? Ask, ask, ask. And where is it established that witches curdle milk? Remember, hearsay evidence is not admissible in court."

Justice Rattle pointed to me with the handle of his mallet. "Does the attorney-*in-fact* need to cross-examine the witness?"

"Yes, sir," I said.

Suddenly I was on, and I couldn't steady the quaver in my voice. I had hardly been aware of the man with the cherry tomato nose, who'd been scribbling down everything said. But I saw him poised with the goose quill in his hand. He was waiting for me.

"Ma'am," I said, after a long moment, "did anyone else look at the pail of milk?"

"No, sonny."

Sonny? I might as well be back in San Diego. "How about your sick friend?"

"You mean Jenny Gaddings?"

"She saw the milk, didn't she?" I asked.

"I brung it to her. Of course she saw it."

"How do you know Jenny Gaddings didn't cause the milk to sour?"

"Don't talk rot! Jenny wouldn't do a spiteful thing like that!"

"Maybe she's the Northampton witch," I said.

A rumble of voices broke out in the room. Justice Rattle banged his mallet for silence and gave me a warning shot.

"Don't be insolent. Jenny Gaddings is not on trial here."

I took a deep breath. I knew that I had an unfriendly audience. The jury watched me perform as if I were some sort of freak, like a talking dog. What was a kid doing asking questions like a magistrate? But Liz looked perfectly satisfied with my performance, and Abigail was smiling like blazes. The cold sweat was drying on my forehead. I was loosening up. All I had to do was play Ichabod Crane as if he were a lawyer instead of a schoolteacher.

"Ma'am," I said, "what was the weather like that day?"

"Common August weather."

A thought jumped inside me, and I probably let a small smile escape. "And how far was it to your friend's house?"

"I never measured it."

"Farther than a mile?" I asked.

"Farther."

"Three or four miles?"

"And a half, I reckon."

It sounded far enough for milk to sour on a hot August day—after she'd taken time to separate a pack of dogs.

"You stated that witches curdle milk," I said. "How do you know that, ma'am?"

"Everyone knows it."

"I didn't."

She gave out a big harrumph. "Then you don't know the first thing about the invisible world!"

Liz passed along an urgent note to me. She wrote it on a yellow pad with a ball-point pen from her purse. Maybe the person beside her thought she was writing with some odd stick of charcoal. The note said: "Hearsay! Hearsay!"

And I said, "Ma'am, would it be correct to say you merely heard that witches curdle milk?"

"No 'merely' about it. I heard it!"

"But you have no proof."

"Witches are too sly to leave proof lying around like dropped handkerchiefs, sonny."

Didn't Liz say to ask and ask? "How about gossip?" I asked.

"What about it?" she answered.

"Isn't it against the law to gossip, even about witches? Don't you have to wear the letter *G* around your neck? I see two such letters in the courtroom."

Deliverance Lankton's face turned red as hamburger. Justice Rattle banged his mallet again. "The witness is not on trial for gossip!" he rumbled. "She has given testimony that Abigail Parsons curdled a pail of milk by the dark glance of her eyes."

"I did not!" Abigail cried out.

I faced the three magistrates. "Sirs," I said, "could not

the milk have soured in the heat? And doesn't it appear that this case is based on hearsay evidence?"

Justice Drywitt was beaming. "It does to me. I think the young attorney-in-fact is wondering if we are not obliged to dismiss the charge."

Justice Rattle straightened his shoulders, lifted his chin, and flashed his profile again. "May I remind you that this is only the first of four charges cried out against the Northampton witch?"

CHAPTER 15

Yellow Cat and Broomstick

While the next witness, a brewer, was being sworn in, Liz whispered to me at a furious pace. You'd think she believed she could educate me in the law in sixty seconds. Why hadn't I asked for evidence to be introduced—the pail of curdled milk, for example? Remember to demand evidence! The charges are ridiculous. See if you can establish motive, Buddy! Call on me as a character witness.

Justice Rattle's voice once again filled the room. "Daniel Gookins, we will now take your testimony. Is it true, sir, the defendant turned you into a yellow cat?"

"Yes, sir."

"Continue."

The witness scratched his neck. "I was delivering a barrel of ale on me cart to Jonathan Burt's tavern when a wheel dropped into a hole in the road and tipped us over and down the slope. I swear that hole wasn't there a moment before. As I was flying through the air, I caught sight of Abigail up in a lightning-struck tree, grinning at me. The moment I touched the ground, she turned me into a yellow cat."

"I didn't!" Abigail cried out.

Justice Rattle shifted his flamethrower gaze at her. "Is it true you climb trees?"

"Of course I climb trees!" she answered.

He gave a small smirk and made a note. "Continue, Goodman Gookins."

"I ran home on all four legs with me tail in the air, and Abigail followed me. And just as I came around the barn, she turned me back into a human, and me yellow fur was gone."

I saw Abigail silently roll her eyes, and then she exclaimed, "You were ale drunk as usual, Mr. Gookins! That's why you didn't see the hole in the road and turned over!"

Justice Drywitt leaned forward. "Did anyone see you as a yellow cat? You have a witness or two, I suppose?"

"No, sir. But that cat did leave me with fleas," Mr. Gookins said seriously. "I scratched for a week."

Liz made me a motion to jump back to my feet. "Sir," I said, "I ask that those fleas be turned over as evidence."

The brewer scratched his neck again and gave the justices a solemn glance. "Afraid I killed the fleas weeks ago, Your Honors."

It astounded me that everyone in the courtroom seemed willing to believe that he'd been turned into a yellow cat. As I slumped glumly toward Liz, I stopped as if fast frozen by a brainstorm. I didn't need to confer with Liz. I knew what to say.

"How do you know it was a yellow cat?" I asked Mr. Gookins.

"I saw me own fur, didn't I?" he answered. "I was yellow all over. Yellow as buttercups."

I gave the jury a glance and turned to the magistrates. I had remembered something from some animal book I'd read as a kid, though it might be news in the seventeenth century. "Mr. Gookins couldn't have seen himself as a yellow cat," I said. "Or a red or green cat either. It's a scientific fact that cats can't see colors. They're color-blind!"

There arose a murmur in the room, cut short by the thunder of Justice Rattle's mallet. "If the public interrupts the proceedings, we'll be caged in here all day. Let us move this case along. The magistrates and I have two more trials to conduct today. We will hear the joint testimony of Abner Green, pig farmer, and Hannah, his wife."

The pig farmer was a bony man with deep dark eyes. He was so anxious to testify he had hardly finished with the oath when he pointed his arm at Abigail and stood there as if posing for his statue.

"That's her! Seen her with my own eyes!"

"Clear as daylight!" his wife added. "I seen her, too!"

"Tell us what you told the grand jury in Northampton," said Justice Rattle, brushing a fly off his nose. I thought of the captain and Mrs. Stebbins still locked up in stocks out front. I hoped someone was keeping the flies off them.

Mr. Green's voice came mostly out his nose and hummed like a tuning fork. "I was walkin' my pigs over by the Parsons place, me and Hannah," he said. "Suddenly here comes Abigail flyin' out of the house, wavin' a birch broom at us. 'Scat!' she yelled, sounding mighty like her pa when he's at home. 'Clear off!' And I said, 'This is a public road, Abigail.' "

Abigail now pointed her own arm at him. "How can you say such a thing, Mr. Green?" she cried out. "Your pigs were rooting in our garden, and not for the first time! My pa warned you!"

"Listen to that wicked child!" Mrs. Green put in. "She hasn't spoken a word of truth since she began holdin' hands with the devil."

"Objection!" I called out, but Justice Rattle was tired of objections and shrugged me off.

"The next minute," exclaimed Mr. Green, "Abigail jumped on that birch broom and rode it straight into the air. Then she swooped down on us, yellin' and carryin' on and scarin' our pigs. Off they run, this way and that, knockin' us backward!"

Justice Drywitt hunched his shoulders forward and grinned ever so faintly. "Thunder and earthquakes! Fire and furies! The wonder of it takes my breath away, sir. You have stated, under solemn oath, that you witnessed a witch riding through the air on a broomstick?"

"I did."

"We did," corrected Mrs. Green.

"And then what happened?" asked Justice Rattle.

Once again the pig farmer pointed to Abigail. "And then she flew at us again, raisin' dust and spinnin' like a whirlwind."

"And out of her pocket fell the book itself!" exclaimed Mrs. Green.

"What book is that?" asked Justice Rattle. Practically licking his lips, I thought. He seemed to look upon the pig farmer and his wife as the star witnesses.

"Why, the devil's own book, sir," she answered. "Old Beelzebub's secret book with names of his witches and wizards writ down in his own hand. And there was Abigail's name in it, big as life."

I didn't need any prodding from Liz and jumped up. "Has the book been handed over as evidence?" I asked.

"Not an unreasonable question," said Justice Drywitt. "Goodwife Green, did you turn over the curious book to the sheriff for safekeeping? It's strong evidence."

"Strong as nails," she said. "But the witches and wizards look after old Beelzebub, don't they? When Abigail saw me lookin' at the book, she shook her fingers and the pages caught fire."

"Then the evidence is in ashes," I said.

"Burned to a crisp," she said, nodding firmly.

"Pity," said Justice Drywitt.

"You may step down," said Justice Rattle.

That finished the charges against Abigail. I looked to Liz for a sign of congratulations on my brilliant legal work so far. But Liz had left the bench and was hurrying out of the room.

How dare she leave me on my own! I thought. Where was she off to? How did she expect me to shoot down that flying broomstick story? It was Halloween make-believe. Looking around at the solemn faces in the room, I wondered if everyone believed the nutcase stuff. Well, maybe not Justice Drywitt. He seemed to know Loony Tunes when he heard them.

But flying broomsticks. I figured I'd better stall for time. Maybe I'd think of something, or maybe Liz would get back in time to help.

"Abigail Parsons," I said, feeling like an actor who had forgotten his lines and had to improvise as he went along, "Abigail Parsons, have you any idea why your neighbors have made these wild charges against you?"

"Clear as the nose on your face," said Abigail.

"Explain it to the court."

Abigail crossed her arms tightly in front of her. "When old Granny Plum was cried out a witch last winter, she got tortured until she confessed."

"That she was a witch?" I asked.

"More'n that. That she had a witch friend in Northampton. She finally nodded her old head that she did—or maybe it just fell forward in a dead faint. Anyway, old Granny breathed her last breath without naming the name of the other witch. And that's what started the mischief."

"Then the witch could have been anyone," I said.

"Everyone was scared that someone would cry them out as the Northampton witch!"

"By a jealous neighbor?" I asked.

"Or someone holding a grudge," she said, and then added, "Like Mr. Green."

"And did your neighbors know," I asked solemnly, "that your grandmother had been tried as a witch?"

"They reminded me often enough."

"Did they believe witchcraft ran in your family?"

"But my grandmother was let off! Free and innocent as a bird."

"But the suspicion of witchcraft kept hanging around, is that true?"

"Aye."

I looked around desperately for Liz. "If you're convicted, no one will have to worry about being arrested as the Northampton witch, is that right?"

"Aye."

"Especially not these witnesses who have cried out against you."

"Especially not them," answered Abigail.

Suddenly Liz came through the door and down the aisle with a broom in her hand.

"Your Honors," she announced in her strongest attorney-at-law voice, "I wish to introduce this piece of evidence."

"A common broom?" asked Justice Rattle.

"A *birch* broom," Liz answered. "Wasn't it a birch broom the witness claimed the defendant rode through the air? I invite the defendant, who has cooperated with this court, to cooperate further. Abigail Parsons, jump on this broomstick and ride around the ceiling. Show us!"

"Show you?" Abigail cried out. "I can't fly around on a birch broom or any other!"

"If you were a witch, could you not ride this broomstick out the window and fly away and be safe from hanging? Jump on, Abigail, and begone!"

"But I ain't a witch!"

"Exactly," said Liz. "I wish to enter this broomstick as evidence that the defendant cannot ride a broomstick, an umbrella, a butter churn, or anything else. She has been falsely cried out upon."

There was a quick rise of voices, and even a quiet laugh or two, but Justice Rattle wasn't seeing any humor in the situation.

"Sit down! The jury will decide whether or not the charges are false or true under the law."

And suddenly, as Liz sat on the bench, I jumped up. Didn't she remember how she'd got the man off who'd been charged with wilting flowers with his evil eye? I'd try the same defense! I hung sort of loose and lanky, like Ichabod Crane in the school play. "Sirs, what if Abigail Parsons did ride a broomstick? You have laws against gossip." I now turned to face the jury. "You have laws against hopping and skipping and kissing on Sundays. *But do you have a law against riding a broomstick?*"

Liz gave me a surprised look. I think she was proud of me. Justice Drywitt erupted with a fit of laughter. When he was able to catch his breath, he said, "Glory to us all! Let the jury be instructed! There is no such law!"

Justice Rattle gave the jury a lofty look. "As there is no further testimony, you men may step into the next room and decide whether or not this child has by wicked and detestable acts shown familiarity with the devil. Should she be hanged and buried with a stake driven through her heart?"

Liz couldn't hold herself back. Up she jumped. "Hanged? Stake through her heart? Not this innocent child! Not like innocent Bridget Bishop, who'll hang from the limb of an oak tree in Salem. The first of many! The centuries ahead will regard Salem as a town gone witch-craft mad. Do you want the name of Boston to send cold shivers through the history books? You will if you take seriously the ridiculous charges against ten-year-old Abi-gail Parsons!"

At that moment Captain and Mrs. Stebbins pushed through the door at the back. Justice Rattle was banging away on his desk to shut Liz up. She'd said what she wanted to say and shut up.

Abigail started toward us, but a constable caught her by the arm. "We'll have to hang on to you, miss."

She cried out, "They're going to put me in chains!"

She made a break for it and might not have made it through the door, but Captain Stebbins cleared the way. In a flash she was gone.

"Ods-bob! Has that fool Rattle convicted her?" asked the captain.

"He tried his best," said Liz. "We'll see."

"Look after her, you and Mercy. Mr. Silvernail has a ship waiting, and the tide has turned in our favor. I'm off to track down the *Laughing Mermaid*. Not a moment to lose! Are you coming along, young Mr. Stebbins?"

CHAPTER *16*

The Sea Arrow

 Once we got outside, it came as no surprise to me that Abigail had vanished from sight. I figured she'd head for a tree somewhere, the way she had last time. Liz thought so, too.

"If the jury decides to hang her, get one of the Silvernail brothers," said the captain. "He'll know what to do."

We hurried past the pillory and the public whipping post toward the harbor. A wind was charging along the street, and the bay was tossing up whitecaps.

I said to Liz, "Keep an eye out for the *Laughing Mermaid* when we come sailing back—if Captain Stebbins can find her. If he can't, you and I had better learn to speak Old English. We'll never get home."

"I don't think you should go, Buddy. I feel uneasy at separating."

"I've got to go."

"Why?"

"Because Captain Stebbins expects me to," I answered. "He's teaching me things."

"I don't think you're going to have much call for climbing up masts."

"I will if we can't get back to the thirteenth floor."

The splintery ship waiting for us had a narrow black hull, two masts, and a name in fancy gold letters across its stern: the *Sea Arrow.*

One of the Silvernail brothers—the one I'd met before, with the tarred pigtail—whipped off his dark hat to give Mrs. Stebbins and Liz a deep bow. "Welcome to my humble ship, ladies."

Mrs. Stebbins gave it an unhappy look. "It hardly looks seaworthy, sir. Fragile as an eggshell."

"Fragile, indeed, madam, but stouthearted," answered Mr. Silvernail. "And fast as a mosquito."

Captain Stebbins nodded. "Splendid, Mr. Silvernail. Is my sextant aboard?"

"Aye, Captain. Everything that came ashore with you has been fetched. As for a crew, I couldn't find a chief mate washed up in Boston and looking for a berth."

"Would you sign yourself aboard, Amos?" asked Captain Stebbins.

I had a quick notion that Mr. Silvernail hadn't looked too hard for a chief mate. "My sea chest's always packed," he answered, and I wondered if he'd somehow heard about the treasure aboard the *Laughing Mermaid.*

Mrs. Stebbins now broke into tears. "Must you leave, dearest John? You've only just returned!"

"And return I shall again, back in command of my own ship."

I was sorry to leave Boston before finding out if the jury would decide to hang Abigail and drive a stake through her heart. At least she had Liz.

The crew came aboard, including Mawkins, the sulky man wearing a bib with the letter *R* on it—for *rogue*. The next thing I knew we were about to cast off, and I decided to get myself out of reach before Liz could decide I wasn't going. In spite of my fabulous, show-stopping performance as an attorney-in-fact, I knew she still regarded me as a twelve-year-old.

A moment later we were waving to each other as the *Sea Arrow* floated free of the wharf. I felt a great sense of excitement. I was going to sea—on purpose this time. It wouldn't surprise me if once we cleared the harbor, the *Sea Arrow* broke out the skull and crossbones. I had a hunch that Mr. Silvernail's splintery ship was a sea rover.

A Gasp of Surprise

It was late afternoon when we cleared the harbor. A large flag of England fluttered at our stern, almost touching the sea. Captain Stebbins set a precise course. I heard him call out to Mr. Silvernail at the huge steering wheel, "South by east by three-quarters east, my friend." You'd think the captain knew exactly where he was going.

It turned out we had a short crew of only seven men, but they managed to get all the sails up now that we were in the open sea. The crack and thunder of the canvas seemed to be music to the captain's ears, for he was all smiles. A crate of live chickens had been loaded aboard, and he suggested I pick out one for dinner, wring its neck, and pluck it.

"Me?" I asked, stunned.

"You're ship's boy, aren't you?"

"Yes, sir," I replied.

How was I supposed to know how to wring a chicken's neck? Or to pluck it, either? Chickens were something wrapped in plastic that you bought at the grocery store.

I managed to pull a wing-flapping chicken out of the crate, but it got away from me on deck. I chased it all over the place, until I ran into a pair of short legs in dirty white stockings. It was Mawkins standing there, chuckling softly.

"Afraid of a chicken, be ye?" he asked.

"Not when they're cooked," I answered.

"Let me have the feathers, lad," he said, "and I'll wring its neck and pluck it for ye. I do like to rest me roguish head on a cloud of feathers."

He had by now cast off the black letter hanging around his neck. Not only did he pluck the chicken, but he cooked it as well, for Mr. Silvernail hadn't troubled to sign on a cook.

I was allowed to eat with the captain and Mr. Silvernail in the main cabin, and it was here I learned that the high seas off New England were infested with pirate ships— English, French, and Dutch. "And they've heard of Captain Crackstone's great good fortune in the Red Sea, John. Be warned."

There was no doubt now that Mr. Silvernail knew about the treasure.

"Be doubly warned." He went on. "While you were away, the crown sent men-o'-war to board the sea rovers, confiscate all treasures, and hang their captains at sea."

The captain looked up and said with a faint smile, "Business partners we are, Amos. But I promise I will not oblige you to hang with me."

"Did you notice, Captain," said Mr. Silvernail, "that we weren't the only ship to clear Boston Harbor?"

The captain wiped his fingers on an embroidered napkin. "Young Stebbins, climb aloft and see if you spy the lights of a man-o'-war in our wake."

I found it less scary to squirrel my way up the ratlines this time. I climbed hand over hand and foot after foot until I reached the platform of the crow's nest. I let out a gasp of surprise that must have carried all the way to the twentieth century.

In the windy darkness I could make out a huddled shadow and ghostly white fingers. And then the figure in the crow's nest spoke.

"I'm hungry."

It was Abigail Parsons.

CHAPTER 18

The Island

 If Captain Stebbins was astonished to see Abigail aboard the *Sea Arrow*, he managed to reveal nothing but a slightly lifted eyebrow.

"My dearest Abigail," he said, for he was her godfather after all. "Child, you are safe for the moment. Young Stebbins, pass the word to the crew that there will be no harsh language spoken, now that we have a lady aboard."

There were two empty cabins, and she took her pick. The chicken had been reduced to bones, but we found plenty of dried codfish and fresh brown bread and cider.

"Where are we off to?" she asked.

I didn't say anything about the Red Sea treasure, but I did explain that Captain Stebbins intended to get back his own ship.

"And return to Boston?" she asked.

"Naturally."

"They'll put a noose around my neck." Her voice rose. "They'll jerk me into the arms of Saint Peter himself!"

I shook my head. "I know for a fact you won't end up on the gallows."

"Puh! You couldn't know such a thing."

"But I do," I said. "I would have noticed it in the family death book. Your name's there."

She stared at me over the top of her cider mug. "I don't hardly believe what Miss Stebbins told me about that place she came from, and you as well. Sandy Egg?"

"San Diego. It's true, Abigail. The worst is what I know about Captain Crackstone. It's him that's going to the gallows, not you. I don't remember what happens to you."

"Who's Captain Crackstone?"

I shrugged and let it go.

Early the next morning the captain himself climbed the ratlines and with his spyglass gazed at the horizon behind us.

"Aye, the man-o'-war's following us like a seabird," he announced to Mr. Silvernail. "Splendid. We mustn't outrun her. Strike the topsails."

Lowering the highest sails must have slowed us a little, for by nightfall we could see the man-o'-war in the distance with the naked eye. But mostly we kept our eyes peeled, Abigail and I, for the *Laughing Mermaid*. She took her turn in the crow's nest. She liked it up there, away from her troubles below.

Meanwhile, the captain assigned Mawkins to further my education. "The captain says to learn ye the canvas, lad. See that un, way at the top? That's the fore-royal, it is. Then you see the topgallant and the fore-topsail, plain as the nose on yer face." For the rest of the day the sea words bounced around in my head: flying jibs and inner jibs and shrouds and buntlines. I wanted to please the captain and tried hard to remember one from the other.

Two nights later we entered a wide river, and there was no longer any doubt in my mind that Captain Stebbins knew exactly where to find his ship.

Early the following morning Abigail in the crow's nest pointed dead ahead and shouted, "Hark! Hark! Is that her? Is that your ship, Captain?"

"Indeed it is!" he replied joyously. "Slowed down by sea grass and barnacles! And there's the *Bloody Hand*, like a mother hen, not far off! Mr. Silvernail, kindly take the wheel."

It was as if Captain Stebbins was now directing a great sea show. All sails set, our black ship headed directly for the *Laughing Mermaid*. Seeing the treasure ship about to be boarded, Captain Scratch raised the skull and crossbones aboard the *Bloody Hand*, as if the blood-chilling sight of it would scare us off. At the same time his bowsprit turned toward us like a sharp lance.

If he didn't change course, he would ram us for sure. But Captain Scratch did change course. For coming up the river behind us, her sails cracking like rifle shots, sailed the man-o'-war.

Captain Stebbins picked up his speaking trumpet and chuckled aloud. "A little surprise for you, Harry Scratch!" he called out across the water. "Ods, my life, if the Royal Navy hasn't caught up with you at last!"

The *Bloody Hand* flew downriver like a startled water-fowl. The man-o'-war tacked about and was soon giving chase. Its gunports opened like garage doors, and brass cannons flashed in the sun. Both ships had vanished from sight downriver before we heard the cannons boom.

Captain Stebbins called Abigail down from the crow's

nest and warned us both not to get in his way as we came alongside the *Laughing Mermaid*.

I saw him draw his cutlass, grab a hanging rope, and swing aboard. Knives between their teeth, Mr. Silvernail and Mawkins followed.

A cheer went up. They were met by Mr. Dashaway, the first mate, and other men of the original crew. Three of Captain Scratch's pirates chose to leap into the river and learn to swim.

"Where are you, Captain Crackstone, you impostor?" shouted Captain Stebbins, roving about the deck. "Mr. Gallows Bird, you public villain! Took my sea name for your own, did you? Impostor, rogue, and infamous murderer, sir! Where are you?"

Mr. Gallows Bird was nowhere aboard.

"He went over to the *Bloody Hand* to parley with Captain Scratch," said the first mate.

Mr. Silvernail and Mawkins returned to the *Sea Arrow*. They transferred fresh food and water to us, and the captain waved them off. It surprised me to see Mawkins take the knife out of his teeth and give the blade a touch to his forehead. It was like a salute. Maybe he wasn't such a bad rogue, I thought, as rogues and pirates go. Maybe all he'd needed was a night's sleep on a feather pillow.

Captain Stebbins took command of his own ship again, and we continued upriver until almost nightfall.

"Mr. Dashaway," said the captain, "I see you were able to persuade Captain Scratch that we had already buried the Red Sea treasure."

"Aye, Captain. And I was leading him to it, slow as a sea slug, like you said. Now, sir, my advice is to find a spot to beach and scrape the hull and repair the leaks."

"We'll bail," said Captain Stebbins.

With the *Laughing Mermaid* once again under my feet, I was walking on air. It was only down a ladder and a hop, skip, and a jump to the thirteenth floor. I could be back in San Diego in time for dinner!

But I'd wait for Boston and Liz. I decided I'd better find a moment to tell Captain Stebbins the truth about us and the twentieth century. He might not believe me, but maybe he would understand once we suddenly disappeared.

We came out into a vast bay with houses crusted like barnacles along the distant shore. The captain found a small, brushy island to his liking, and he began taking sightings.

That night, after Abigail had gone to bed, he called his old crew together under the yellow candlelight of his cabin. If he noticed me in the shadows near the door, he didn't tell me to scat. Maybe cabin boys were of so little importance they became invisible.

"Gentlemen," he said, "when it comes to treasure, some men are wise, some are otherwise. The man-o'-war is bound to be back looking for us, eager for pirate loot. Let us be wise. Let us now truly bury the Great Mogul's treasure."

"But where are them will-o'-the-wisp jewels?" asked the bosun, tightening the yellow scarf around his head. "We searched everything aboard but the wind in the sails."

There were nods all around. Captain Stebbins held up his hand.

"Did you search the laughing mermaid?"

"Our figurehead?" asked the sailmaker.

The captain nodded. "Aye, that fetching mermaid hidden under the bowsprit that you can't even see from the riggings. Have you forgot she was there?"

A sailor in rags burst into a laugh. "That Red Sea treasure was right under our clumsy feet all this time?"

"Indeed," said the captain. "She's hollowed out and stuffed like a sausage full of diamonds and rubies and pearls. Is that not so, Mr. Dashaway? In Madagascar, when you men were wild ashore, did we not busy ourselves all night?"

"We did, sir."

Said the captain, "We'll bury our lovely mermaid here, on this flyspeck of an island. Take down the figurehead, mates, and lower away a boat."

I saw it all. I watched as the wooden mermaid was rowed to the island. I saw the sparks of shovels glint like fireflies in the darkness. I heard whispers. I could make out the mermaid being buried—buried as reverently as a great queen.

I saw it, but I could hardly believe my luck.

I was watching pirates bury their treasure!

CHAPTER 19

The Map

 We were several days beating our way north, catching winds and losing them. We were so slow in the water that even the seabirds drifted ahead of us. We saw no sign of the man-o'-war.

The captain pointed out Nantucket and then Cape Cod to Abigail and me. The closer we came to Boston, the more anxious Abigail became.

"You sure that book of yours said that Abigail Parsons didn't get hauled up by the neck?" she asked.

"I don't remember exactly what happens, Abigail. But you won't hang."

"I won't, not if I stay run off, will I? That's what I'll do."

She helped bail out the ship, as if to assure herself that she'd have a ship afloat to hide in. We all bailed, and even the captain himself took turns emptying wooden buckets over the side.

Several times when I was down below, I found myself staring into the heavy darkness to the rear. The thirteenth floor lay there, waiting. Waiting for Boston so that I could grab Liz's hand and show her the way back.

I couldn't wait much longer to tell Captain Stebbins the truth. When I brought him his dinner, he was doing something to his speaking trumpet. "Hold your finger here, young Stebbins," he said.

I held my finger, and he pounded a rivet into the trumpet, and then another. I could see at once that he was wrapping a sheet of thin copper around that speaking tube of his. And I could guess why.

"Is that the treasure map, sir, scratched on the copper?" I remarked boldly.

"It is, indeed," he said, without the least attempt to conceal what he was doing. It was as if he took for granted that any cabin boy of his would show him absolute loyalty. But he had another reason. "Lad, what if I should slip?"

"Slip, sir?"

"Aye, tumble down a ladder. What if villains ashore set upon me and knock the sense out of this head o' mine? And my memory along with it, as happened to Harry Scratch in Bristol? So here's the longitude of our wooden mermaid, and her latitude, and if I get the senses knocked out of me, I charge you with the duty of refreshing my memory."

Then I saw him drop a silver coin between the double sides of the speaking tube and seal it in. He gave the trumpet a shake and seemed pleased to hear the rattle of the coin.

"One ship's trumpet looks like a thousand others," he explained. "This one now has a voice. There can be no mistaking it."

"Aye, sir," I said, surprising myself. Aye? I was beginning to talk seventeenth-century English like everyone else.

"Young Stebbins, watch what you say along the docks of Boston. Treasure maps fever the imagination of rogues and villains, you know."

"You needn't worry about me, sir," I replied. "Once we reach Boston, I'll be going home."

"And where exactly is that, lad?" asked Captain Stebbins. "You did try to tell me, but I didn't get a straight fix on it in my mind."

"I'm from California."

"Of course," he said with a small chuckle. "That's twelve miles south of London, I believe. Or is it over the hill from Canton, China?"

"We're from years and years in the future, my sister, Liz, and I," I said, persisting. "We kind of tumbled back into history. But I can show you the twentieth century."

I'd come prepared with the small tape recorder that had been knocking about my backpack. "Speak into this, sir. It'll imitate your voice."

"Do what?"

"Say something. Shout or sing. Anything."

He was game. "Avast!" he called out. "Belay that, you muck-eyed fools. Rascals, stand aside or you'll feel the blade of my cutlass! I'm Captain John Crackstone, and may God of infinite mercy be merciful to your soul!"

I rewound and played it for him.

He jumped back when he heard the jack-in-the-box voice. He listened to it twice more and then gave me a twinkling look from under his eyebrows. "I saw a fellow in Jamaica could throw his voice and make it come out of a chicken," he said. "Well done, young Stebbins. I didn't see your lips move. Not the merest twitch!"

I gave up trying to explain. I thought of showing him the pencil flashlight in my bag, but I knew it would be hopeless. He'd look for lightning bugs.

CHAPTER 20

Escape

 "Anchor!" shouted Captain Stebbins through his speaking trumpet. "Drop anchor!"

With a loud rattle of chain, the ship's anchor splashed into Boston Bay. We tugged like a dog on a leash, about a quarter of a mile from the wharves.

I saw a ship's longboat separate itself from the fishing boats unloading along the Public Dock. Seamen were rowing two passengers—a woman and a boy about my own age with his coat glistening with brass buttons.

The captain gave them a wide wave, and they waved back. It was Mrs. Stebbins coming to board the *Laughing Mermaid*. As they drew closer, I knew I'd seen a picture resembling the boy. Could that be Tobias Stebbins, the captain's son, who'd posed for the painting hanging in the captain's cabin? Must be, I thought.

But where was Liz?

Even as the ladder was let down for Mrs. Stebbins, I saw Abigail duck out of sight. She was trembly over the news that might be waiting for her ashore.

Captain didn't pause to ask if it was Sunday or not. He swept his wife into his arms. And she melted away into tears.

"Oh, John," she sobbed. "You're alive after all!"

"Of course I'm alive. Hello, Tobias. My dear son, I trust you had a good voyage."

"A splendid voyage, Father."

But Mrs. Stebbins's eyes were still awash. "John, you were hanged!"

The captain looked perplexed. "What nonsense is this? Strung up?"

"A man-o'-war anchored in the bay three days ago. They had caught a pirate off New York and hanged him from the mainmast."

"Captain Crackstone?"

"So they said," exclaimed Mrs. Stebbins.

"Gallows Bird," remarked the captain airily. "Poor fellow, he must have hoped to escape the gallows again, as Captain Crackstone. That murdering villain had already used up cat's lives, all nine of them, under his own bloody name. Good riddance—both of those gents."

My face must have glowed up with a jack-o'-lantern smile. The death book at home had croaked an impostor!

"What about Abigail?" I asked, unable to restrain myself any longer.

"The child has disappeared," said Mrs. Stebbins.

"Did the jury decide she was a witch?"

"The jury was brought to its senses and declared her to be a ten-year-old girl, and nothing more." Mrs. Stebbins went on. "But that sweet child has vanished from the face of the earth."

"I'll tell her," I said.

"You mean she's aboard? Run off to sea?"

"Hiding. I'll find her."

"Let me," said Tobias. "She'll be surprised I'm back." And off he strode, looking proud of his coat lit up with brass buttons.

The captain, meanwhile, shouted to Mr. Dashaway to go ashore for pumps. "And bring back some fresh hands to man them. This crew of ours has bailed out half the Atlantic Ocean."

"Sir," I said, "I'd like to go ashore as well, to find my sister."

Mrs. Stebbins gave a little gasp. "We just came from visiting her, child."

With a rush of fear I asked, "Is she sick?"

"Nay." Mrs. Stebbins shook her head, her lips tightening. "Your sister is locked in the prison house."

"What for?" I blurted out.

"On a charge of witchcraft."

I was struck speechless. Finally I croaked, "What's she supposed to have done?"

"They say she augured the goings-on in Salem Village."

"Augured?"

"Told the future. At Abigail's trial she said that Bridget Bishop would be hanged as a witch from the limb of an oak tree. Yesterday Bridget Bishop was hanged from the limb of an oak tree."

"I'll get my book and show them all!"

I got my backpack. We all climbed into the boat—except Abigail and Tobias. He hadn't yet been able to find her.

When we tied up to the Public Dock, large codfish were being flung from the fishing boats. They sailed through the air like huge flying fish and piled up in slithery heaps.

Making its way through all the noise and confusion, a procession was marching along, led by the buckle shoes and long, flapping coat of Justice Rattle.

I saw Liz just behind him, her chin lifted and defiant. Her hands were tied at her back while a constable in ragged brown stockings urged her along.

"Buddy!" she shouted, seeing me through the flying fish.

I rushed forward, dodging around Justice Rattle. "Liz! Are they going to hang you?"

"If they can! They brought me down here for the water test!"

"The what?"

"The water test for witches! They're going to tie me up and throw me in the bay. If I drown, it'll prove I'm innocent. If I float, it'll prove I'm a witch!"

"That's nuts!" I shouted. "You lose either way! If you don't drown, they'll hang you!"

As if I were a pesky dog nipping at his heels, Justice Rattle reached for my collar to fling me aside. "King James himself approved the water test! Stand clear," he demanded.

"Look, sir," I shouted. "Salem and the witch trials made the history books. That's how my sister knew about Bridget Bishop! It says everyone around here went crazy as bedbugs. You're hanging innocent people! I'll show you—"

"Buddy!" Liz cried out sharply. "Keep your trap shut and that book closed! They'll hang you as a wizard!"

"What book?" asked Justice Rattle, turning his gaze on me as if I might be a rare new butterfly to add to his collection. "Let's see your book! It sounds in need of burning."

Captain Stebbins stepped between us and motioned me away with his concealed hand. But just then heads began to turn, and fingers began to point to the *Laughing Mermaid*.

Waving her arms and yelling her head off, Abigail had revealed herself up in the crow's nest of the *Laughing Mermaid*.

"Hark! Hark!" she shouted across the water. "We're sinking! Leaking something terrible!"

My heart dropped. The thirteenth floor! It would soon be at the bottom of Boston Bay.

Captain Stebbins leaped into the longboat to return to his ship. There might be time for Liz and me to get aboard.

"Liz! Run for it!"

The constable took a tighter grip on her rope. Justice Rattle stretched his arms like the wings of a bat, as if to protect his prisoner.

I ran forward through the crowd. I don't know what Liz thought as I disappeared before her eyes. But I knew what to do. I knew how to be a wizard.

I ducked behind a pile of dead cod and dug the tape recorder out of my bag. I turned it on and shoved it down the throat of the biggest codfish I could find.

As Justice Rattle and his committee advanced, I sent the fish slithering to his feet. And it began to talk.

"Avast!" said the fish. "Belay that, you muck-eyed fools."

Justice Rattle took a staggering step backward. His eyes sprung wide open. A talking fish?

"Rascals," the cod continued, "stand aside or you'll feel the blade of my cutlass! I'm Captain John Crackstone, and may God of infinite mercy be merciful to your soul!"

Here was witchcraft. Here was the real thing. Here was the voice of a dead man scaring the daylights out of Justice Rattle and his committee of witch finders. They scattered like frightened crows. The fish began speaking Spanish.

"*¡Es excelente! ¡Es estupendo! ¡Es magnífico!*"

"Come on, Liz!" I shouted, catching the rope dragging from her wrists. We beat our way to the end of the dock, and I cried out to Captain Stebbins not far off, "Wait for us!"

He waved me back. He had no time for cabin boys now.

I undid the knots to free Liz's wrists and told her to jump. "When the *Laughing Mermaid* goes down, the thirteenth floor will sink with her."

We jumped, but we didn't have to swim it. Mr. Silvernail came along in a small boat and fished us out of the water.

C H A P T E R *21*

Return of the Ghostie

 As we approached the *Laughing Mermaid*, Captain Stebbins was already long aboard. He must have determined there was no saving the ship. I saw him up on the quarterdeck with the copper speaking trumpet at his lips.

"Abandon ship!" he called out. "Save yourselves, mates! Into the boats, lads. Abandon ship!"

As the first men came scurrying down the ladder and into the harbor boats gathering to help, Liz and I were trying to scurry up.

We reached the main deck, and I grabbed her hand. "Follow me. And trust me."

But she saw Abigail and pulled away, and they hugged. "You're free, Abigail!"

"I know. Tobias told me. Thank you grandly." She turned a smile on me. "And thank you grandly, too, Buddy."

"Don't mention it. Liz," I added urgently, "this ship is going to sink!"

I pulled her away. At the rear hatch I paused to give a

Mawkins-like salute to Captain Stebbins. He paused on the quarterdeck to give me a sharp look. "What did you came here for?"

"Just to say good-bye, sir," I answered, and suddenly choked up. I knew I was never going to see Captain Stebbins again.

"Tobias," he shouted, "see that Abigail gets safely into one of the boats."

"Aye, Father."

"Young Stebbins!" exclaimed the captain. "You heard the order! The bottom's stove in. Abandon ship!"

I waited until he turned his back. "Good-bye, sir," I said. Then I pulled Liz into the hatch and down the ladder.

I could hear the leak bubbling up below, and as we started down the next ladder, it grew darker. I fished out my pencil flashlight. It had gotten wet, but it still worked. I saw black water rising in the bilge. And rising out of the water at the foot of the ladder was the tangle-haired sailmaker with his sea chest on a shoulder. When he saw me, he flew into a rage.

"I knew you was a dredgie, bringin' us evil luck!" he roared. "Aye, and look at ye now, with ghostie lights coming out of yur fingers. Back up and out of me way!"

"Step aside!" I shouted.

He drew his knife. "Jonah's luck, that's what ye are!"

I jammed the flashlight all the way into my mouth and bared my teeth as if it were Halloween. It would make me look like a vampire about to bite.

He fell back in white-eyed terror. "Save me wretched soul!" he exclaimed.

I pushed past him down the ladder. Liz followed. I grabbed her hand again, and we waded around toward the rear of the bilge. The sailmaker went clattering up the ladder. He had cost us seconds of time.

The water was already almost to my shoulders. I flashed the light around, looking for the thirteenth floor. The ship was rumbling and squealing as it began breaking up. Beams cracked like chicken bones, and planks were falling around us.

I pushed aside a floating beam and felt the top of a low door. My heart gave a lift. "Here it is, Liz!" I shouted. "The thirteenth floor!"

But the door had no knob.

"Liz! We've got to pry it open!"

I got my fingers under the top edge of the door, and Liz did the same. We pulled. Tons of seawater were pressing against it. The thirteenth floor was stuck tight! I could feel the planks of the door beginning to twist under the strain of the collapsing hull.

We pulled again. But we were no match for the power of the sea.

This ship would go down within seconds, I thought. Liz reached out for my hand. She must have been thinking the same thing. Water was swirling up around our necks.

Suddenly the sea blew out the door.

And we blew out with it.

Liz and I went tumbling head over heels. There was a moment of howling blackness and then silence. We were as wet as codfish, but we had returned to the thirteenth floor. My heart was beating something crazy. We were practically home.

"What do we do now?" Liz asked.

"Press for the elevator," I said.

CHAPTER 22

The Treasure

With the three-hour time difference, it was still morning in San Diego. The lawn needed cutting, the mailbox was full of junk mail, but home had never looked so good. It stood right where we had left it, on the hill overlooking the bay, waiting for us like a shaggy old friend.

I watched a passenger jet roar in low to land at Lindbergh Field. A gray navy destroyer was heading out to sea, and I could hear a TV playing next door. I didn't have to pinch myself. It was the twentieth century.

Liz opened windows to let a breeze blow through the house. She listened to the phone messages while I checked my room, just to make sure it was still there. I emptied my wet backpack. My Spanish book was a sodden lump. I'd have to study again and make up the test.

I crossed to my dad's room and got the dented old speaking trumpet.

When I returned downstairs, Liz had turned on the

TV set to catch up on the news. "Did you hear that, Buddy?"

"Hear what?"

"Some clods out on the desert burned a pile of green library books."

"Green?"

"They believe it's the devil's favorite color."

I wanted to laugh and shrug it off, but I couldn't. It was as if Justice Rattle had slipped through the thirteenth floor with us and was loose in the twentieth century.

"No important phone messages?" I asked.

"School wants to know where you've been. I'll write you a note."

"What'll you say that they'll believe?"

"I'll think of something." And then she said, "Buddy, we've a very good offer on the house."

I shook the trumpet in the air. "But we've got the captain's treasure map. What if no one ever went back for the Red Sea treasure? It'll be ours! We won't have to sell the house."

But even as I said it, I knew something was wrong. I'd shaken the trumpet, but where was the sound? Where was the rattle of Captain Stebbins's coin? Wasn't this the same speaking tube?

"But look, sis," I said, "I was there when he pounded in extra rivets. And here are the extra rivets. This *must* be the same trumpet!"

I got my dad's tin snips and just about ruined them cutting the rivets. A thin, curled sheet of copper came loose, and a tarnished coin tumbled out onto the carpet.

I smiled victoriously. "The coin was only jammed!" I exclaimed.

"After three hundred years it's allowed."

Now that Liz could see the map for herself, she began taking the possibilities more seriously. "You were there when they buried the plunder, Buddy? Actually there?"

"Actually there!"

"This map doesn't look as if it's ever been unrolled before." She ran her finger along the copper. "Is this a river?"

"Sure. And we came out into this bay. And there's the small island. That's where the mermaid is buried."

"What do you suppose these numbers are? They're scratched in very clearly."

I looked down at the markings.

Lat 40° 41'
Long 074° West 4'

"That's easy," I said. "That's got to be the latitude and longitude. The little circles mean degrees. The apostrophes mean minutes. Didn't you ever have geography?"

Liz got up, crossed over to the phone, and picked up the telephone book. After a moment she punched out a number.

"Who you calling?" I asked. "The airlines? We could fly back to the East Coast tonight!"

"Hello, Coast Guard," she said into the phone. "Could you tell me where forty degrees and forty-one minutes latitude is, by zero seven-four degrees and four minutes west, please?"

"Liz!" I practically screamed. "That's a secret! You want everybody to know where to dig?"

"I didn't say anything about a treasure, did I? Maybe we're looking for someplace to take a vacation."

"Sure." I groaned.

It took the Coast Guard a couple of minutes to get back on the line. Liz had a pencil ready, but she never wrote down anything. Didn't the island have a name?

"It's got a name all right," she said after hanging up.

"Well, spill it," I said.

"You've heard of Bedloe's Island."

"Bedloe's Island," I said.

"It must ring a bell."

"Not very loud," I answered. "Ring it again."

"How about the Statue of Liberty?"

"What about it?"

And Liz said, "It's on Bedloe's Island, standing right over the treasure."

I felt as if I had been flattened under a ton of bricks. A ton? It wouldn't surprise me if the Statue of Liberty weighed ten zillion tons. Unless Captain Stebbins had already got to it, the Red Sea treasure was going to stay buried forever. Maybe longer.

We still had the debts our parents had left, but we were able to hold on to the family house after all. That coin Captain Stebbins used for a rattle may have been common enough three hundred years ago, but it turned out to be a New England threepence. It was rare to the max. Only two others were known to be still around. So we got big bucks for it and paid the debts.

That was a huge favor Captain Stebbins did for us. I think of him a lot, and since he didn't die on the gallows, I corrected the family death book. It was only when I stumbled across his son Tobias's entry that I discovered what happened to Abigail. She married him in 1699! They begat a lot of wonderful kids and terrific descendants. Especially Liz and me.

When Liz wrote my school excuse for being absent, she said, "Visiting relatives."

 Not all of this story came leaping out of my imagination. Some of it is the goggle-eyed truth.

When my wife's grandmother died, an old family history fell into our hands. We discovered that my wife was descended from a Massachusetts woman tried as a witch in the late seventeenth century.

I was fascinated. But as my novels have a comic surface, I wasn't sure it was material I could develop into book. I doubted that I'd be able to find a laugh anywhere in early New England.

I was wrong. I stumbled across a ship's captain who returned to Boston after years at sea and was promptly arrested for kissing his wife on Sunday. It was against the law, as well, for kids to run on the day of rest or to hop, skip, and jump.

The age of witchcraft coincided with the great age of piracy, and I discovered that the men of New England were up to their buckle shoes in sea roving. That's what pirates are doing in this novel.

When it came to charges of witchcraft, I discovered that nothing was too absurd. A man offered as evidence that his feet went suddenly hot in the presence of a villager accused of witchcraft. A woman claimed under oath that she had seen a neighbor turn herself into a bear. A man said his spurs "came jingling after him through the woods." Witnesses swore in court they had watched village women riding on broomsticks.

That such charges were taken seriously in court is their principal amazement. While the famous witch trials in Salem, Massachusetts, sent fewer than two dozen people to their deaths, they were the sobering climax of a nightmare century of witchcraft madness. Toward the end of the terror even street dogs were charged with being witches!

It was a century not kind to women, who were the principal victims. In Old England and across Europe, many thousands of pious mothers and church-devoted grandmothers were hanged from the gallows or, like condemned books, burned in public bonfires. Men also perished in the rampage.

Children? Ignorance and superstition are loose cannons. Children perished, too.